"The wonder of Stacy Barton's fiction
characters. There are hard, dark, vivid sto
plenty of struggle and ambiguity as wel
is that of the author, her stories and the
the way."

PHILIP F. DEAVER, author of *Silent Retreats,* winner of the Flannery O'Connor Award for Short Fiction

"Stacy Barton's considerable genius is that she looks at the world we all look at, but sees what the rest of us are unwilling to see. And she doesn't flinch. The disarming beauty of *Surviving Nashville* can be, at times, quite breathtaking. Here is the art of few words and powerful resonance. Stacy Barton's brilliant collection will haunt you. It's courageous, honest and smart."

JOHN DUFRESNE, author of *Louisiana Power and Light,* a *New York Times* Notable Book of the Year

"Stacy Barton's stories tug at the cozy blankets around my mind and soul. She makes me think long, hard thoughts with her spare yet lovely prose. I am a voyeur, a gaper, hungering for more with each vignette."

CHRIS-MARIE WAVE, coauthor of *Conversations at the Girlville Diner*

"Stacy Barton's stories fly from dark to light and back again in depicting the human condition. Her words sing to accompany her characters in their varied journeys that touch the gamut of readers' emotions. Through it all there is the never-spelled-out but felt sense that the writer knows that beyond the dark glass she'll find Light and the answers to the unanswerables."

LAWRENCE DORR, author of *A Bearer of Divine Revelation*

"Reading *Surviving Nashville* was like listening to the perfect album—each song complete in itself, but when you listen from beginning to end, you end up singing out all the pain and grief and love you didn't know you had in you. I love these stories that poured out of Stacy Barton's soul. In languid prose, pain and faith mix and find their voice in mothers, sisters, best friends, summers and food fried in cast iron skillets. *Surviving Nashville* is full of stifled cries, devastating events and moments of beauty. Each story released in me a cry of pain and the glimpse of a tiny miracle."

ALICE BASS, author of *The Creative Life*

SURVIVING NASHVILLE

SURVIVING NASHVILLE

Short Stories

STACY BARTON

WORDFARM
LA PORTE, INDIANA

WordFarm
2010 Michigan Avenue
La Porte, IN 46350
www.wordfarm.net
info@wordfarm.net

Cover Image: Getty Images
Cover Design: Andrew Craft

USA ISBN-13: 978-0-9743427-8-8
USA ISBN-10: 0-9743427-8-5
Printed in the United States of America

First Edition: 2006

Library of Congress Cataloging-in-Publication Data

Barton, Stacy, 1964-
Surviving Nashville / Stacy Barton.—1st ed.
p. cm.
ISBN-13: 978-0-9743427-8-8 (pbk.)
ISBN-10: 0-9743427-8-5 (pbk.)
1. Sisters—Fiction. 2. Suicide—Fiction. 3. Nashville (Tenn.)—Fiction.
4. Domestic fiction. I. Title.
PS3602.A8425S87 2006
813'.6—dc22

2006005476

P 10 9 8 7 6 5 4 3 2 1
Y 12 11 10 09 08 07 06

for Todd

Contents

Periwinkles

THE SUMMER STRETCHED OUT LONG before us. I think we believed it would go on forever like the endless line of sea and sand. Our noses pink and strong legs brown, we ran like colts in the surf.

"Elaine! Sammie!" my older sister called, laughing from the jetty in the surf. "Periwinkles!" The three of us ran with buckets to scoop up the dainty creatures. We dished and funneled the tiny shellfish from bucket to bucket.

"Violet!"

"Salmon!"

"Blue!" we shouted, as we mined our priceless gems and separated them by color into Styrofoam cups.

As the Atlantic sky grayed in the evening light, the sea became our looking glass; we modeled the ocean's treasures like mermaids. But our jewelry was temporary, and, with childhood ceremony, we released our periwinkles into the tidal pool. Then Sarah Jane, Sammie and I lounged on our tummies in the long shadows and late waters until Mamma called us in for fried potatoes, snap beans and canned pears atop mountains of cottage cheese.

■ ■ ■

"I got the pears at the grocery, Mamma," I called as I plopped the plastic bags onto the kitchen table. I tossed my keys on the counter and stepped out to the porch.

"Dole?"

"Yes, Mamma."

I leaned over and kissed her cheek. We sat in the stillness of evening and let the waves talk for us. Mamma only weighs ninety-four pounds, but she is still stronger than I am. I said so to Sarah Jane once, and she laughed.

"For Pete's sake, Elaine, Mamma's old."

But Sarah Jane and Mamma don't speak. Sarah Jane married a doctor, moved to a big white house in Atlanta, and has two boys at prep school. Sarah Jane forgets what it smells like here.

I miss Sammie; she could always make us laugh.

■ ■ ■

"Elaine, watch," Sammie said, suppressing a giggle. "Who am I?" She staggered across the porch, leaned against the screen door, and took a long swig of her sweet tea, after which she drawled, "My, my, but you do look lovely this evening. I do believe the sunset matches your eyes."

For some reason, the idea of Mamma's eyes matching a sunset sent us all into adolescent hysterics.

"Girls! Pipe down; I can't hear the game!" Mamma's boyfriend, the subject of Sammie's parody, called from the TV room.

"We're sorry, sir."

Sammie and Sarah Jane just buried their faces in the chaise lounge and laughed harder. I shot them worried looks and waited to see if Mamma would visit us on the porch. Sure enough, we heard her rise from the divan.

"Let me freshen your drink, darlin'." Mamma's voice purred with gin, and on her way to the icebox she hissed through the screen, "Don't mess with this one. He's gonna be our ticket out of here. He does business in Miami!"

Sammie rolled her eyes, fluttered her hands like a debutante, and whispered, "I didn't know Prince Charming sold tires." We responded with such a fit of laughter that we had to run off the porch and into the freedom of the dunes.

■ ■ ■

"Well, are we gonna eat or not?"

"Of course, Mamma. Would you like to eat now?"

"Yes. That woman you have comin' in can't cook worth a hill of beans. She's a Yankee. Can't fry a potato, keeps fussin' about cholesterol. I say we all got to die—and fried is the way I want to go."

That made me laugh, which pleased Mamma. We went into the house, and I pulled out the pan. "I've got all of tomorrow left before I go home, Mamma. What would you like to do? Wanna go into town?"

I filled the big skillet halfway up with oil like Mamma likes and went to the crisper for the potatoes.

"I will not go into town and have those ladies talk behind my back and feel sorry for me."

I cut the milky potatoes into wedges and waited for the oil to heat up. "How about June or Elsie, Mamma? Would you like to visit them?"

"I would not. Do you have enough oil in the pan?"

"Yes, Mamma."

"Don't cut the potatoes too big."

"No, Mamma."

■ ■ ■

When I went off to college, I remember feeling like Sammie was the lucky one.

"Sooooo, tell me about your family." Sharon spoke sweetly and curled her blonde hair around her finger. "I mean, we're roomies and all now, practically sisters."

"Well—"

"My daddy was the mayor of Savannah," Sharon interrupted. She paused for effect. "Twice."

"It was just me and my sisters. No mayors, just a tire salesman from Miami that stayed on for a while."

"Oh," Sharon said. "That's nice."

We sat on the edge of our dorm beds and hesitated. Eventually, Sharon recovered.

"So you live with your mother?"

"Uh-huh."

Sharon's Georgian diplomacy served her well. "You have gorgeous skin; I bet your mother is lovely."

"Mamma is beautiful and strong. The only one of us that could ever stand up to her was Sammie."

"Well, beautiful is good. Where is your sister?"

"Which one?"

"Sammie," Sharon said and smiled, certain she had come upon a safe topic.

"Dead," I said. "She killed herself when I was twelve."

The mayor from Savannah got Sharon a new roommate.

■ ■ ■

"Mamma, where are the little pink dishes?"

I smoothed the summer cloth on the kitchen table.

"I stacked them above the icebox," she said with an injured sniff. "I don't entertain anymore. No one cares to come see me."

"I do, Mamma," I corrected her and pulled out the glass dishes to please her. I laid a bed of iceberg on the bottom, then a scoop of cottage cheese with a Dole pear half on top as the crowning glory. Mamma had long believed that individual salad dishes were a mark of high society.

I took the tuna salad out of the fridge, placed the fried potatoes on the table, and poured Mamma her Diet Coke. Mamma drinks Diet Coke now. No more gin, the doctor had said, absolutely no more gin. So Mamma drinks Diet Coke—with a little rum.

"Well," Mamma began, "have you found a man yet?"

"Oh, Mamma, don't start."

Mamma sniffed again and took a sip of her Diet Coke. "I don't see how you can live in New York City and not be able to find a man."

"I'm not looking, Mamma."

"Good grief, of course you are," she said. "You're over forty."

I waited, hoping the conversation was over. Sammie would have walked out onto the porch and lit a cigarette. Sarah Jane had just stopped coming. I sat there.

"Maybe if you lost a little weight or did your nails or something. Men like that, you know."

"Yes, Mamma, I know."

I lacked the courage to tell her that was precisely why I didn't starve myself or get my nails done weekly. I looked over as she examined her last remaining beauty, red lacquered nails. They were too bright against her blue-veined hand, but they were Mamma. She really had been beautiful. She certainly received the attention of many men. My father was just not one of them.

■ ■ ■

"Okay girls, we're going into town!"

Mamma gathered the three of us together and waved a ten-dollar bill. "Everyone gets ice cream and a new bottle of nail polish!"

We all squealed in delight and tumbled into the back of the blue Ford like puppies. Mamma had us singing and laughing all the way to the drugstore. Mr. Johnson chuckled as we chose our nail color and licked our cones. We were bouncing home and singing another chorus of "Oh, Susanna" when Mamma blurted out between verses, "Your father is gone."

I decided then that I would never wear nail polish.

■ ■ ■

I left Mamma dozing in front of the news and went for a walk on the beach. The July breeze was almost too warm, but the sun was sinking; it was my favorite time of day. I wet my toes in the edge of the sea and looked for periwinkles. There were none. I walked all the way to the jetty, sat on the rocks, and watched the sunset turn my skin the shellfish colors of my childhood. The smell of the sea and the summer heat were too much; I closed my eyes and breathed. I allowed the memory.

■ ■ ■

Mamma and the tire salesman were drinking martinis in the living room. Sarah Jane had gone back to college. Sammie had argued with Mamma and gone out, puffing on a Marlboro. I was sleeping on the porch because my room was hot.

A truck pulled up, and Sammie hopped out laughing. The pick-up honked and drove away. I pretended to be asleep and hoped that Mamma and her salesman had gone to bed. But I could hear Johnny Carson through the screen door. Sammie was not even trying to be quiet. Her high heels tapped across the porch, and she sang a disco song and swiveled her hips because she could. She was beautiful like Mamma. And so alive.

Mamma lay passed out on the divan, and I thought for a minute that we would all escape, but the tire salesman got up and came out onto the porch.

"Who do you think you are? You little tramp! How dare you storm out of here and have the nerve to come back at this hour?" His attempt to whisper was thwarted by the weekend martinis. I shut my eyes tighter, but I couldn't make him go away.

"I'm not afraid of you," Sammie said and stood taller. The salesman and I both knew she wasn't.

I watched from my Girl Scout sleeping bag as the salesman snorted and reached for the doorway to steady himself. I prayed he would pass out. Instead, he grabbed Sammie. I was afraid he would beat her, and I couldn't move. But the salesman didn't beat her.

"I'll teach you," he said, and he shoved her onto the chaise lounge and pulled up her summer skirt as he fell on top of her. She started to scream, but he hit her hard across the face with the back of his hand. His foot was at an odd angle, giving him leverage as he fumbled with his trousers and ripped off Sammie's panties. Mamma must have heard the commotion, because she came out to the porch just as her salesman entered Sammie. Mamma just stood there, stuck to the porch floor like the salesman's thick foot. Finally he stood and buckled his pants. Mamma and the salesman went to bed.

After I saw Mamma's light go out, I crept out of my sleeping bag and went over to Sammie. She was trying so hard not to cry. I reached out to stroke her head, and she flinched at my touch.

"It's just me, Sammie, . . . Elaine." She didn't move, but she let me smooth her hair. I tried to fix her skirt and button her blouse, but she was bigger than me by two years and unable to help. I sat with her for a long time on that chaise lounge, but she wouldn't talk or even look at me. My eyes got heavier and heavier.

I didn't mean to leave you alone, Sammie.

I woke up in the morning on the chaise lounge, and Sammie was gone. Her panties were on the floor in a lacy heap, and there was blood on the cushion. Mamma was frying potatoes for the salesman. They burned. Mamma forgot the oil.

They found Sammie three days later down by the jetty; her body was so bloated from the sea that we had to keep the casket closed. Sarah Jane came home from college for the funeral and spoke to Mamma for the last time.

"How did Sammie die?" Sarah Jane asked.

"She drowned" was all that Mamma would say. I had to tell Sarah Jane the rest when Mamma wasn't listening.

The salesman went back to Miami; he had been with us for two years.

■ ■ ■

I looked out at the sea and remembered three little sisters running in the summer sun. I remembered Sarah Jane and periwinkles and Sammie before the salesman. I remembered Mamma before gin: how she could laugh like music and how we all wanted to be like her. I inhaled the irony with the salt air.

Leaving the jetty for the sand, I discovered the tide had brought periwinkles. I followed their translucent colors back to the house and stood on the porch until the sunset faded. Tomorrow night I would be back in Manhattan where the smell of the sea couldn't reach me. I would call Sarah Jane from my apartment, and we would cry.

"Come on, Mamma." I turned off Jay Leno. "Let's go to bed."

Jimmy

HOW HE GOT HIMSELF CAUGHT under that damned car is beyond me. But he did. Trying to change the oil. Lousy brother of mine—he still owed me twenty bucks. He must've gotten all pumped up watching NASCAR on the cable channel, decided his old Pontiac needed some attention, and headed off to the Kmart Plaza.

The Kmart Plaza—wasn't he something? Some men die for honor, some in war, but my brother died a drunk in the Kmart Plaza stuck beneath a 1979 Grand Prix.

He was an ass anyway. Couldn't hold down a job for anything, and he thought more of his Old Milwaukee and that scraggly dog than anything else—except maybe Daddy's Pontiac.

After I settled things at the hospital, I went over to his trailer. I don't know why I didn't wait a day or two. Maybe I wanted to see if I could find a twenty-dollar bill and even things up. Anyway, I pulled up in the gravel and climbed out of my truck. I whistled for the dog, but he didn't come. I fumbled with Jimmy's keys and stepped inside.

Stale Marlboros and the familiar smell of canned Spaghettios greeted me. I tried to laugh but it came out like a small sob. I threw open the door to prove he was gone, took three strides across his living room, and thrust my hand inside his cookie jar. Three singles and a pair of quarters. Damn. I shoved a pile of laundry off the sofa, sat down, and wiped my face on my sleeve.

The storm door was still open, and I could see out across the street. A couple of little kids were driving toy trucks around in the dust and hollering now and again over who got the dump truck. At one point, the big kid hauled off and slugged the little one in the shoulder. He got the truck.

I closed my eyes for a minute and let the sun go down on all that was left of a long day. Something wet touched my hand. I jumped, but it was just the dog. He wanted supper. I wondered if he knew Jimmy was dead.

I got up, rummaged around in the cupboards, and found a can of dog food. Canned food my brother fed this mutt, while he scrounged to buy himself Spaghettios with food stamps. I pulled open a drawer for the can opener and slopped the food in a bowl. A fat woman in a threadbare nightgown called the kids inside for supper. Their screen door slammed. I grabbed a beer and sat on the stoop and drank it while the dog ate.

Nothing had changed. Not in three years. Same old dog, same old trailer, and the same old brother who owed me—only he wasn't there to scrap with, and I never really wanted the dump truck anyway.

The dog looked up, and I patted his head. We sat in the dark until I could hear the television through the window next door. I stood up, closed the trailer, and walked on the gravel back to my truck.

The dog followed me.

I looked at his scruffy face and thought about my leather seats. Finally I opened the truck door and patted the passenger side. He jumped up and grinned at me. He reminded me of Jimmy.

I got in, and we drove away.

On Tuesdays

ON TUESDAYS, MRS. LORETTA DARLING came outside and carefully walked between two perfect rows of red geraniums. When she reached the sidewalk, she turned exactly to the right, walked all the way to Second Street, then turned again. She picked her way around the block until her last turn brought her back to the little white house with red geraniums. Then Mrs. Loretta Darling went inside and closed the door.

Mrs. Loretta Darling had lived at 43 East Mulberry Street for forty-seven and one-half years. She had grown senile and had "taken to her bed" for the last dozen or so—except on Tuesdays.

The assortment of ladies that Mrs. Darling's son had coming in to care for her knew to come after ten o'clock on Tuesday mornings, when Mrs. Darling would be back under her afghan wearing her black pumps and a flowered house dress.

Charles was the handyman and the gardener. Charles had been there the longest. The turnover rate for the inside help was much greater; many of the ladies found Mrs. Darling's Tuesday outings just a little too disturbing.

"It's Tuesday" was all Charles ever said, and he kept the geraniums red and the little house clean and white.

As the Tuesday outings kept up, most people in town began to have Charles's attitude. The doctor found something in a medical textbook somewhere about how geriatric senility could reverse the effects of agoraphobia or something like that, and so people learned to accept her Tuesday morning strolls. In fact, school children often learned to distinguish the days of the week by Mrs. Darling's bobbing head.

One summer Mrs. Darling's weekly promenade became particularly significant. It was the summer that Melissa Albright moved into the brick house on the corner. Melissa was eight years old at the time, and Mrs. Darling was in her final year of Tuesday strolls.

No one in town knew exactly where Melissa's family was from. But they were suspicious. A large moving van had unloaded an endless supply of tidy boxes, and a veritable army of workers unpacked and situated all day, so that by evening one could peek into the windows of 13 East Second Street and see a home that, by all appearances, had always been. There was even a pot of pink petunias by the door.

The next afternoon, Mr. and Mrs. Albright and Melissa arrived. In a taxicab. First Mrs. Albright emerged, then Mr. Albright, carrying the little girl. They went inside and closed the door. After that, only Mr. Albright left the house. Every morning at exactly five o'clock, he walked to the station in town and rode the train for one and three-quarters hours to Tulsa. He was a lawyer.

Folks started talking down at the Five and Dime.

"Have you seen the child?"

"Heard she's sickly—poor little thing."

"Her mother called and asked if we could send a boy around for her grocery order. Lord, you think she's ever gonna come out?"

There was one consolation felt by the people of Elmswood: the Albrights had not installed air conditioning. Though the windows all had eyelids of lace, their sashes were up morning and night. Howard's wife, Betty, who ran the counter at the Five and Dime, said she knew for a fact that the Albrights had moved from up north for the dry Oklahoma air, on account of Melissa's breathing problems.

Charles was the only one in town who had seen the child. Seems Mr. Albright had heard that Charles did odd jobs for Mrs. Loretta Darling. He inquired as to Charles's availability and hired him to help Mrs. Albright around the house while he was off in Tulsa doing whatever it was that lawyers did.

So Charles trimmed Mrs. Darling's hedge and kept the Albrights' plumbing in fine working order and was attentive to both households. The first few days spread into weeks, and then a month or two went by. While the Albrights were still considered strange, there was the men's softball team contending for the county title that year and the church ice cream social to plan, and soon the citizens of Elmswood only commented occasionally on the new folks.

Until Melissa's face began to appear in her bedroom window. On Tuesdays.

At first no one noticed it was on Tuesdays that her face appeared, but Betty, down at the Five and Dime, began to keep track of who had seen the child and when.

"Last week, Betty, day before the men played the Waverly team. I remember because I came down for some Clorox to whiten James's socks."

"I believe it was just the other day, Betty. I saw the little child's face at the curtain."

"She's such a tiny thing—don't look near eight. Looks more

like my Cindy, and she's barely five."

"Come to think of it, Betty, I believe it *was* Tuesday."

Meanwhile, Mrs. Darling continued her morning stroll, right past Melissa's bedroom window. Mr. Albright kept to his 5 a.m. train, Mrs. Albright called in her grocery order, and Charles tended to knobs and cranks and pipes and lawnmowers and smiled when folks hinted at his odd employers.

Betty, down at the Five and Dime, kept watch. If it hadn't been for her, the curious events of that summer might never have been chronicled. Charles, certainly, was not inclined to talk.

Melissa Albright was a very sick little girl. As the summer progressed, Betty noticed the doctor came by more and more frequently, but all she could get out of him, due to his professional propriety, was that the child would not make it to Halloween.

"Devoted parents, those Albrights," he'd say, "that Mrs. Albright almost never leaves the child's side."

Betty did learn from the doctor that sometimes Mrs. Albright would ask Charles to sit with Melissa so she could have afternoon tea in her backyard. He said Charles had made a real nice patio with flowers and a garden bench and such. He said Charles was real tender with the girl, held her hand, and told her country stories that sometimes made her smile.

The Friday before the Fourth of July picnic, Mrs. Loretta Darling's son came to town. He hired a new nurse, visited the various stores where he kept accounts, and paid his bills. He asked Charles to check the roof and bought the necessary replacement shingles. He had the doctor come by to conduct a physical examination of his mother. She was expected to live another decade or so. Then he made a deposit at his mother's bank, gave Charles a new book of checks, and left before noon on Monday—well before the picnic began or his mother went on her Tuesday walk.

Down the street at the Albrights' house, Melissa begged

to go to the picnic. Of course, this was strictly forbidden, but Charles managed to draw the curtains back and prop the child up on pillows so that she could see a bit of the festivities from her window, as the town square was at the end of Mulberry Street. When the child got too tired to watch, Charles described the events in great detail—without looking. There had been the same three-legged race, softball championship and watermelon-eating contest since he was a boy. Folks say that Mr. and Mrs. Albright sat and listened to Charles's tales of storybook picnics as attentively as their dying daughter.

That evening, Charles carried Mrs. Darling out onto her front porch to watch the fireworks. Of course, she never opened her eyes. Charles had brought her out every Fourth of July for the past twelve years, because her son had once told him in passing that his mother loved fireworks.

The next morning, Mr. Albright took the five o'clock train. At nine o'clock Betty opened the Five and Dime, and Charles went to work. He knew not to disturb Mrs. Loretta Darling on Tuesdays until ten, and so he bought a Little Golden Book about a puppy from Betty and walked to Melissa's house on the corner. Mrs. Albright let him in, and, while he read to Melissa, Mrs. Albright had her morning tea on the patio.

What follows is the story that Betty loves to tell to anyone who will listen. Even today, some twenty years later. Of course, a few details may have been added or embellished by Betty's strong imagination, but there is no challenging the outcome.

As Mrs. Darling came around the corner, Melissa's breath began to stick in her throat. As Mrs. Darling's heels clicked onto Second Street, Charles became alarmed and hollered for Mrs. Albright.

For the first time in twelve years, Mrs. Darling stopped.

Inside, Melissa grew gray without breath, and Mrs. Albright came running.

Outside, Mrs. Loretta Darling left the sidewalk and marched straight to the little girl's window. Melissa saw her and, through panicked gasps, reached out the window. As Loretta thrust her bony hand through the lace, Melissa grabbed it. At that moment, Melissa inhaled deeply and fainted back onto her pillow. Loretta turned and walked the wrong way back to her house. Charles and Mrs. Albright stood transfixed.

"There was no explaining why Mrs. Loretta Darling died in her bed that very afternoon," Betty would go on to say. "Or how on that day Melissa was miraculously cured of her terrifying lung malady."

"Amazing."

"Unbelievable."

"A miracle," people would say.

But if you asked Charles, he would look up from whatever he was mending and say, simply, "It was Tuesday."

Hail, Mary

MY VERY BEST FRIEND IN all the world was Mary Katherine. She was Catholic. There were seven children in her family, and every single one of them had red hair. There were so many kids in that house that her mamma didn't even bother with bed sheets; they just slept three or four to a bed right across the top of the mattress. Mamma said that wasn't Christian, but Mary Katherine didn't seem to mind.

We were Nazarene. There were only a very few of us in St. Margaret Parish, Louisiana. We didn't drink, and we didn't smoke, and we put out clean linens every week. We never swore, and we never worked on Sundays. There was only me and Mamma, and we ate meat every Friday. At Mary Katherine's there was never enough food, too many kids, and Mary Katherine's daddy drank whiskey. Mamma said they'd go to hell for drinking and for praying to the Virgin Mary, but I thought it was nice at Mary Katherine's house. There was a lot of laughing there.

Mary Katherine and her mamma helped me sneak into the movies sometimes. In general my mamma believed movies were the handiwork of the devil. Last summer we saw Fred Astaire and Ginger Rogers. My mamma would never have approved of that one on account of its having dancing. Mamma definitely didn't believe in dancing. I thought it was beautiful and couldn't imagine what could be wrong with twirling around to gorgeous music. I couldn't imagine God would hate me for it, but I said a quick prayer at the shrine for the Mother Mary in the rosebushes at Mary Katherine's—just in case.

It was a beautiful place, that shrine. I could just feel heaven when I was there. *Hail, Mary, full of grace. Our Lord is with thee.* She had the sweetest expression on her face, and her hands were stretched out among God's roses. I imagined that if she weren't made of stone she would just break out dancing. *Blessed art thou among women, and blessed is the fruit of thy womb, Jesus.*

Mary Katherine wasn't so sure that the Mother Mary danced, but she said I should imagine so if it helped me with all the guilt I felt for disobeying my mamma's church. If I wanted to get near to God, I suppose I would just go out under the stars and be quiet and wait to see what God actually had to say. But I'd never heard of anything like that, so I just sat through the services with Mamma and heard how we were all going to burn in hell if we weren't extra careful. I spent most of my time tracing the pew in front of me with my eyes.

Saturday was to be a very special day. We were going to see *Gone with the Wind*. Mary Katherine and I had been waiting for weeks. We had every last detail planned out. We told my mamma that there was an additional Girl Scout meeting over at Laura Lane's house to discuss the upcoming cookie sale. I planned to wear my very ugly Girl Scout uniform because Mamma couldn't possibly imagine that I could do anything terribly evil in a Girl Scout uniform. Of course, I would have on an extra shirt underneath, but I simply must bear the disgrace of going to the movies in my Girl Scout skirt. It couldn't be helped. But I didn't care so very much because I was going to see Vivien Leigh!

By Friday night I was so nervous I couldn't eat my okra, and Mamma started to worry I was taking sick. So I stuffed my mouth full of the little slimy things, and when Mamma wasn't looking I spit them into my napkin. I hoped God wouldn't get angry at me for wasting, and I said a special blessing on the poor heathens in Africa.

I could hardly sleep all night. In the morning Mamma asked why my color was so bright, and I said because I was especially excited about winning the badge for the top Girl Scout cookie sales. Mamma didn't look exactly convinced, but before she could think of anything else to say, I kissed her goodbye and ran out the door. I would have to say another prayer to the Holy Mother for lying on the way to the movies, but I didn't even care.

There was a decided thrill in going to the Ascension Palace Theater downtown. Even though we were seeing a matinee, they had the popcorn machine running and all the lights on just as if we were going to a nighttime feature.

Mary Katherine and I showed up red-faced and breathless; we had run all the way from the corner where her mamma dropped us off to escape being seen by anyone who might tell my mamma where I was. We slipped into the ladies' room to cool our faces with a little water and remarked about how we just might faint from the excitement of it all. Mary Katherine had snuck a tube of her mamma's lipstick, and we giggled as we painted our lips movie-star red.

We bought our tickets and mooned over a large *Gone with the Wind* poster as we counted out our change for hot buttered popcorn. I squeezed Mary Katherine's arm, and we walked down the aisle of the theater like brides.

I liked to sit close to the front and clear in the middle so I could feel like I was actually inside the moving picture with all those beautiful people. The Ascension Palace was the one place in the whole parish where I could believe.

The lights went dim, and the red velvet curtain parted, and Mary Katherine took my hand. We were beholding the very opening of *Gone with the Wind* itself. We hardly breathed, it was so beautiful, and we held each other all the way through. We were weeping by the final scene and positively hugging, and I couldn't quite help myself—I kissed Mary Katherine on the lips. She was warm and salty and surprised, but she kissed me back, and for a moment we were Rhett Butler and Scarlett O'Hara, and St. Margaret Parish fell away, and God loved the Nazarenes.

Then it was over. We giggled, wiped off our lipstick, gathered up our popcorn bags and little change purses, and headed for the door. Suddenly, I was stone. There was my mamma in the doorway to the theater looking as though she hated me more than life itself, and all the beauty just slipped right out of me.

Mamma sent Mary Katherine directly home and didn't speak to me in the car—except to tell me she was ashamed that I was her daughter and that to save my soul from burning in hell for eternity I was never to see Mary Katherine again. I didn't even cry.

Later in my room, I traced my lip with my finger and remembered my best friend in all the world and wished I had been born a red-headed Catholic to a family that was going to hell for whiskey and prayers. I remembered Scarlett O'Hara in *Gone with the Wind,* and Mary Katherine's movie-star lipstick and all those glorious sleepovers without sheets. I considered asking the *Holy Mary, Mother of God,* to *pray for us sinners now and at the hour of our death. Amen*. But I was a child of a devout Nazarene, so I laid on top of the hot summer covers and closed my heart to God.

The Death of Rosie and Grace

IF I HOLD MY BREATH and sit still like this, them sweet little things in pearly white jest let me be. I learnt it from Clarence one Thursd'y durin' our Social Hour. Miss Jenny's girls, all perky and smilin', had us lined up like we was in a church. We jest sittin' in our chairs fillin' up the damn parlor. Ain't no parlor anyhow, what with leavin' room for all them wheelchairs. The parlor about like the garden this place is named after—jest some plastic sofas and a ugly brown console TV from Mr. Jeffery's garage. He be proud of that thing, too, like he so benevolent or somethin'.

So we sittin' there waitin' to be *socialized*—that what Miss Jenny call it—when I notice that Clarence over in the corner ain't got nobody buggin' him with fake smiles and perkiness, and I start to wonder how come that is. So I watch him all mornin', and he be pretendin' he off thinkin' about his past. Past about all we got, I guess, but I know Clarence, he about as sane as anybody here, includin' Miss Jenny and Mr. Suited-up-Jeffery. But them little perky girls in white, they scared of Clarence. I seen that after a while. 'Cause when he start a singin' or rollin' his eyes, they jest start avoidin' his corner. So I decided, after that, *I* was gonna sit over by Clarence and pretend to be senile too.

My girls, they come see me every Sund'y after church. Wanda and Winnie. They is good girls. Every other week they make they grandkids come along. Oh, them babies—they jest like candy. They got the sweetest skin and pretty smiles with all they teeth, and I be so proud 'cause I got babies for visitors! I know some of them other old coots jest want to get they hands on my babies, so I always say, on *those* days, that I want to go out into the courtyard. Ain't much of a courtyard—we no royalty here—but the air is better: no piss smell. They got about four benches and some plastic roses in a concrete vase. It look like they preparin' us for a tacky funeral.

Frid'ys we get fish, 'cause Mr. Jeffery, he a *Catholic* man. Don't think I ever knowed no Catholic man. Cleaned once for the nicest Catholic lady, though. Irish woman. She worried me a little. Had these pictures and little hangin' things of the dead Jesus all about her place. In *my* church we be spendin' way more time on how Jesus be rose up again. We all need a good story with a fine endin', and they ain't no better endin' than comin' back from the dead! Anyway, we eat fish sticks on Frid'ys, 'cause Mr. Jeffery's a Catholic man.

Mr. Jeffery, he in charge of this whole place here, and he all full of hisself, like a man his age always is—busy tryin' to make somethin' of his life and all worried about who noticin' what he done. Clarence and me, we speculate on him now and again. Mr. Jeffery got two suits and four ties. I know what day of the week it is by what he wearin'.

Now, Miss Jenny, she sweet. Sweet as the day is long. She so sweet that when she put it all together for the whole lot of us, she too much for me and Clarence. But we like her; she our Social Director. Miss Jenny, she barely more than a child, and she smell better than anybody here.

But it *is* on account of her we got sorry-ass entertainment here at The Gardens. Miss Jenny don't mean it, but I don't know what she think we like. Last Thursd'y we had a fat accordion player in here. He was wearin' short pants and everthin'! That man had gray hair, and he was wearin' short pants! Lordy.

Clarence and me, we been beggin' Miss Jenny for a little jazzy somethin' on Thursd'ys, but she jest smile and pat us like *she* the grandma and say she workin' on somethin' special for me and Clarence.

Thursd'y is a good day, usually. Miss Jenny has us do occupational therapy, which means we get to paint. I painted me about sixteen ceramic dogs by now. My family say they don't want no more "if that be all right with me" and "see how sweet they is in your room, Mamma." So I runnin' me a whole collection of painted ceramic dogs along my windowsill.

One Thursd'y, in the middle of paintin', Rosie and Grace, they jest pitched forward right into they paints. Rosie and Grace is twins. They married brothers, too, but they died—long time back, Rosie say. At first, I thought maybe they both looking hard at they dogs or somethin', but pretty soon me and Clarence knew they was gone. They jest up and went together, like everthin' else they ever did.

Now why they went and called an ambulance is beyond me. We is all *old* here. But they did. And so the lights, they came a-flashin', and the portable doctors with they big suitcases came trompin' in, and they started poundin' on those old ladies' chests and shootin' 'em full of stuff to make they heart start again. Well, they work and work and holler orders at everybody, and I notice Miss Grace. Her dress all hiked up and showin' her Depends, and I thought how proper a lady she and her sister was, and I jest couldn't stand it. So I yelled at all of 'em to stop. Only it come out like a howl—a big long howl comin' out of a china dog. Clarence seed me, and he knew what I was thinkin' so he started up, too. This made Mr. Jeffery mad ('cause by now he out and all important in the action), so Mr. Jeffery made a couple of them little girls in white wheel me and Clarence out into the courtyard and leave us there, so they can go back inside and help those big men try to pump life back into bodies that don't want it no more.

Now, Mr. Jeffery, he don't love Rosie and Grace. Far as I know, Mr. Jeffery only love hisself and his blue suit. Maybe fish sticks, I don't know. And those big men, they jest doin' what they trained to do, but nobody seem to think what maybe Rosie and Grace wanted. I try to think who come to see Rosie and Grace, but I couldn't quite remember it. I thought maybe they should be here.

Clarence, he decided it too much for him, so he start doin' the senile thing. I push my chair up to the window, and I see Miss Jenny inside jest standin' there, cryin'. Mm-hmm. Cryin'. And I think maybe she startin' to understand that losin' our life ain't what we afeared of at all. It be *this*. This right here. And I start to hopin' that maybe she gonna do somethin' to stop this craziness, but she jest standin' there watchin' Rosie and Grace try to slip away while those big men and Mr. Jeffery try to bring 'em back. Then Miss Jenny, she look up and catch my eye through the glass, and we jest cry together over all the dignity slippin' away with them twins.

After that, we don't paint no more on Thursd'ys. Miss Jenny decide we should plant flowers.

Bach Tu's Sadness

ME AND MY LITTLE BROTHER, Paulie, went with Bach Tu to the Cheap Shop. Actually, sometimes we asked her to go just so we could hear her say it. She said Cheap Shop like she was chewing it. Me and Paulie loved it.

The Cheap Shop was like a giant garage sale; it smelled like mothballs, and you could get anything you wanted for less than a dollar. They had rows and rows of used belts all lined up in rainbow order. Bach Tu always got something—a shirt for her girls or maybe a vegetable strainer. She even bought us little things if they only cost pennies. Once, Paulie wanted to buy a big old soup pot for a quarter, but Bach Tu wouldn't let him because we would have to carry it all the way home. We always walked to the Cheap Shop. You could get there in five minutes from our house if you didn't stop. I think the Cheap Shop maybe had another name—I don't remember because they tore it down to make room for the

TG&Y, but to Bach Tu and me and Paulie, it was always just the Cheap Shop.

Bach Tu came to our house the year Mamma tried her hand at being a feminist. Daddy said far be it from him to stand in the way of progress, and, if Mamma wanted to go to work, well then, he was all for it. So Mamma went to town to sell ladies' dresses and lipstick at the Woolworth's, and Daddy got Bach Tu for us. By summer Mamma'd had enough of her retail career; she quit the Woolworth's and came back home to me and Paulie. But not before I had felt Bach Tu's sadness.

Bach Tu was one of the boat people that the Texas Christian Ladies were sponsoring from Vietnam. Mamma didn't usually like the Texas Christian Ladies, but she told Daddy she would make an exception on account of helping out somebody who was less fortunate.

Daddy always teased that he couldn't remember if her name was Bach Tu or Come From. I don't think Bach Tu thought his jokes were very funny, but she nodded a lot and smiled anyway.

■ ■ ■

Once Mamma took us along to get Bach Tu. She lived in an apartment house where you could drive right up to the door and park. Paulie and me waited in line with the other cars while Mamma went up to the door. When Bach Tu opened the door, I could see her two little girls standing inside. They were wearing pink and purple sleeveless shorts sets from the Woolworth's. They looked especially shiny and new, not like the ones from the Cheap Shop, and I was sort of proud for them—except that it was wintertime, and we were all wearing our Christmas car coats.

I remember how Bach Tu's girls looked in that one little space before the door shut. Their leaving faces stood still on top of their bright outfits, and their sleeveless arms hung down plain at their sides.

■ ■ ■

Bach Tu was like a strange secret. She had cinnamon skin and peeking eyes, and when she talked or sang she sounded like the birds. Bach Tu didn't smell like Mamma. Mamma smelled like the rosewater in the little bottle that sat on her vanity. Bach Tu smelled like something spicy and strong—kind of like summer clover when you pinch it.

Some days Bach Tu would stand in our kitchen, and a long look would cover her face. The air around her seemed to wait quiet with her. And then, suddenly, she would go back to doing whatever it was she'd been doing before the long look came. I always wondered what she was thinking on those days.

■ ■ ■

Once Paulie and me came inside from riding bikes and found Bach Tu crying on the bathroom floor. She just sat folded on the floor in her yellow gloves with a toilet brush in her hand. Mamma had come home from the Woolworth's and was sitting on the toilet with the seat down. Later Mamma tried to explain about Bach Tu's sadness.

Mamma said it made Bach Tu sad to clean toilets that day. Paulie and me asked her why, and she said because it reminded Bach Tu that she had been like a princess in Vietnam, and princesses don't clean toilets. Mamma said when the men with guns came, Bach Tu and her family had to run away on a tiny boat crammed with people. They couldn't even take suitcases. Mamma said Bach Tu had had a baby boy in her tummy that was halfway grown, but it died on that boat.

The next day Bach Tu didn't come to our house, and Mamma didn't go to town. She played Johnny Cash records on the stereo and used Pledge on the furniture. It was lovely. I pretended to have a sore throat and got to skip school, and Paulie and me laid on the couch with bed-pillows and watched *The Price Is Right* with Mamma fluttering all around us.

I closed my eyes and tried to imagine being on a tiny boat with so many people. I wondered if they talked and, if they did, if they sounded like the birds. I scooted so close to Paulie on the couch that he got mad and went to the kitchen to ask Mamma for chocolate milk. But I was just trying to feel what it would be like to be so close to someone you couldn't move. I wondered how they went to the bathroom, and if they had to go in their clothes. I wondered if Bach Tu's baby felt it when he died, and if his little body came out in Bach Tu's clothes, too. Mamma said he would have been a year old by now.

Mamma came in with a tray for Paulie and me full of chocolate milk and egg salad sandwiches cut in triangles. I smiled at her. I imagined that Bach Tu's girls were smiling in their pink and purple shorts sets too. I imagined away the stillness in their tilted eyes and hoped they were having something lovely on a tray with their mamma.

■ ■ ■

A few weeks later Bach Tu started planning a special dinner. She took me and Paulie with her to a place in town to get stuff they didn't sell at the IGA. This store wasn't by Mamma's Woolworth's. This store was way *past* the Woolworth's, and it was squished behind a laundry. It smelled like going fishing inside, and everyone had peeking eyes and bird voices like Bach Tu. It sounded loud and clangy and almost scary if you weren't used to it just a little bit.

Bach Tu picked out some long fish with heads and whiskers, and a wrinkled man wrapped them up in newspaper. Which was fine with me, because they looked slimy, and one of them was watching me with his googly eye. She put some funny jars and vegetables I had never even seen before into a straw basket she brought. You couldn't fit a shopping cart into a little place like that.

When Bach Tu went to pay, I just stared at all the little bottles of things lined up behind the counter. They made a tower all the way to the ceiling. There were little tins with red dragons on them, big brown bottles with dancing letters, and little paper boxes, mostly white. They belonged there, like the colored belts at the Cheap Shop.

Bach Tu made bird music with the smallest woman I had ever seen; she had to stand on a stool just to reach the cash register. Bach Tu counted out a bunch of coins and two paper dollars for the lady on the stool, and we left.

Me and Paulie both hoped we'd get to go there again, but it wasn't likely, because Bach Tu had gotten special use of her husband's car for the day, and she would have to leave early to take him to work. Bach Tu's husband worked the night shift all the way on the other side of Harris County.

On Friday my stomach was like a tilt-o-whirl. Bach Tu was finally making her special dinner for us, and her whole family was coming to eat at our house. I had picked out a bunch of my things and lined them up on my bed. I wanted to give Bach Tu's girls something, but I couldn't decide what. I had two shirts, two dolls, and two stuffed animals Daddy won me at the fair. I had two necklaces and two hair bows, but I wasn't sure if their thick black hair would fit right in them. Finally, I put everything away and took out the macramé bracelets I made last year at summer camp.

Bach Tu wouldn't let me and Paulie anywhere near our kitchen that day. She giggled with her hand over her mouth and shooed us out whenever we tried to sneak in. She chopped and hummed and stirred bubbling things on the stove all day. Mamma came home a little early, set the table, and put on her Johnny Cash record and a fresh dress. Paulie and I cleaned up, too. Bach Tu went into the bathroom, and, when she came out, she was wearing the most beautiful thing. It was a long, tight dress covered with red flowers that tied fancy around her middle. Her hair was up special with pearly sticks. She had some black lining on her eyes and very red lipstick. She was completely beautiful. Paulie couldn't stop staring, so I poked him in the ribs to make him mind his manners. But he yelled, and Mamma sent us into the other room.

Even though it was still chilly outside, I found a shorts set from last year and put it on. It was sleeveless. Daddy and Bach Tu's family came in their cars at the same time, and so it was all busy as they came inside. Bach Tu's girls stayed quiet behind their daddy, but Bach Tu made them come out to meet me and Paulie. When she said their names were Amy and Jenny, I tried not to look disappointed. I had hoped they would have faraway names like their mamma. I took them right away to my room and gave them my bracelets. They nodded a lot, and I think they almost smiled.

The smells from our kitchen were not Mamma's pot roast or fried chicken. They kind of stung my nose a little. But I didn't want to be a baby, so I sat right down between Bach Tu's girls and glared at Paulie so he wouldn't say anything stupid to hurt Bach Tu's feelings. Paulie wasn't even looking at me; he was busy figuring out how to work the chopsticks Bach Tu had brought him.

Daddy said the blessing, and then Bach Tu brought in the food. My favorite was the Garden Rolls. Garden Rolls are little tubes of dough with meat and salad inside (I guess the salad part was how come they were called Garden Rolls). They were soft and sweet and crunchy, all at the same time. Bach Tu said there was sweet peanut sauce on them, but I never did find any peanuts.

Daddy laughed right out loud at how much rice Bach Tu had made; we never ate rice before. But that night Paulie ate three helpings and acted crazy with the chopsticks, and Bach Tu's girls started smiling.

I looked over at Bach Tu. She was perched up tall like a princess in her long red dress. Her bird voice sang above the sadness, and her arms floated like wings as she served us hot tea in cups without handles.

Secrets

MAMA DIED ON A SATURDAY. At least she had the sense to do that. It was August and hotter 'n hell.

Mamma believed in Sunday burials—said you were a heathen if you were buried on any other day of the week. Personally, I always thought it was just one way you could be sure to have the most mourners. Those poor folk, stuck in church anyhow, may as well mourn your death as not. 'Course, not everybody goes down to the cemetery, but certainly nobody in Clydesdale misses your going out if you're buried on the first day of the week. Not as though anyone's death could go unnoticed in a little town like Clydesdale; pretty near everybody brings a covered dish to the house that's in mourning. But just the same, we count heads here. Mamma had 248 at her going out.

"She looks lovely, Susan, just like herself."

"Oh, Sue, honey, didn't they do a fine job making her up?"

"My, my, but she is *still* one of the best-looking women in Clydesdale."

I swear that last one actually made Mamma swell with pride.

■ ■ ■

"George, what the hell are you doing?"

"Just cleaning out, Suzie."

"Well, stop it. Leave everything on the bureau to me. Honestly! Go outside and see if you can help Sam with the garage or something."

"All right, Suzie, don't fuss. You sound like Mamma."

That sat me down. Right into the chair at Mamma's dressing table. I looked at myself in Mamma's mirror, all her little jars of beauty lined up in front of me like an army of femininity. I, of course, had inherited my father's naval looks.

I opened every one of her jeweled bottles and smelled. Mamma had very expensive taste when it came to beauty aids. I smeared a little of each on the underside of my wrist and was torn between setting up a shrine and throwing every one of those damn bottles out the window.

Instead, I went downstairs and made some sweet tea. Drank four glasses before I called the boys in for lunch. We had chicken salad coming out our ears, it being summer and folks not wanting us to have to heat up the oven. So chicken salad is what we had. Chicken salad and sweet tea.

I felt sorry for my brothers. I felt sorry for myself when I thought about it. We had this big old house full of childhood nightmares and chicken salad. It was August to boot. Seemed like it was always August.

Sam came in and slapped me on the butt. I threw a dish towel at him.

"Wanna spike the sweet tea?"

"I do not."

"Aw, come on, Suze. We need a little life in this old house. I'm dying out there in that pisshole of a garage. You can't believe what kind of crap George and I are sifting through. Let's just call old Martha at the church and tell her she can have it all, and then let's the three of us take Mamma's money and fly to Vegas or Tahiti or something. What do you say, sis?"

"I say you may spike the sweet tea. We are not going to let Martha Waylan and those old biddies sort through our family belongings without checking through them ourselves. I can barely hold my head up in this town as it is."

George came in, and we ate chicken salad, and I felt like Mamma.

■ ■ ■

The story goes that, some time back, there was a gentleman farmer raising horses out here who thought naming our town Clydesdale would be prophetic. Problem was, the Navy bought up his horse farm and built a training base. So now we got squids instead of horses, but it still says Clydesdale on the map.

Sam and George and I were all born in early June—conceived in late August by a variety of the incoming naval trainees. Squids, we called them. Mamma called them God's Countrymen. She swore she never intended to have so many husbands—said God had just made her unable to resist the fresh young men that arrived in Clydesdale each summer. All we had of our daddies were some pictures Mamma took out on the porch. There was a picture of Mamma and a squid for each of us.

The Augusts I remember followed the same pattern without the addition of any more babies except George. However, by the time Sam and I were in junior high, George had started kindergarten and Mamma's looks had faded. So Mamma swore off the entire Navy, made friends with Martha Waylan, and became a devout Baptist.

■ ■ ■

"Susan! Where are you?"

"In here, Sam."

"Where in here?"

"In the dining room. I got the pictures out. Where's George?"

"I sent him to the store for some beer."

We sat cross-legged on the floor and pulled pictures out of the cardboard box Mamma had kept at the bottom of the china cupboard for as long as I could remember. They were a warp of memories that brought everything back I had been trying to forget.

"Hey, look at you in this one, Suze! Nice hair!"

"Yeah? Well wait till you see this one."

"God, Suze, did I really wear that?"

"Easter, Sammy. We all looked like that at Easter. Mamma thought it was cute."

"Hateful woman."

"Hey, found any of George yet? He'll love this shit."

"Yeah, look here. It's the birthday we got him that green bike."

"Look at this one, Suze. It's the three of us all lined up on the porch!"

Sam pulled me over, and we looked at the picture together. Sam was growing tall, and I was sprouting breasts. It was the August George started school and Mamma quit the squids. I could feel Sam's warm breath on my shoulder.

"How did we survive, Sam?"

"The best we could, Suze."

Sam accidentally brushed my breast as he put the picture

down. It froze him like a small child shamed by an evangelist. I scrambled to my knees, pretending to be intent on gathering up the pictures, but old sensations flooded me, and I started coming loose inside.

Suddenly the door slammed, and George came in with the beer. He stood still for a moment, staring at us. Then he set the beer down on the dining room table and walked out onto the porch without saying anything.

"George! We found a picture of you with that old green bike." I jumped up, looked back at Sam, and dragged the box to the porch.

We popped open the Old Milwaukee and started drinking. There wasn't much of a breeze, but the cans were cold and the sun was down. Nobody spoke. We finished off a six-pack under the yellow porch light before George started shuffling through the pictures like a garage sale shopper hoping for a bargain. He kept trying to put them in some kind of order.

"Hell, George, you're not going to be able to make any sense out of our childhood. Just give it up and have a beer."

"I got a beer, Sam. Suze, this my daddy or yours?"

"Shit, who cares?" Sam said, "They were just Mamma's squids, George. They weren't daddies."

Sam argued with George, and I leaned back and laughed. I noticed the sound of my own voice and how old the porch light was and wondered how long it had held a yellow bulb. I left my head back and watched the moths bump into the light over and over again and wondered why God made such stupid creatures.

Later, up in Mamma's bedroom, I slipped off my shirt and stood naked in front of the mirror. I ran my fingers over my nipples till they stood up, and I wondered if God would send us all to hell.

■ ■ ■

"Shoot, Martha, how should I know what Mamma did with her sewing machine? Yes, I'll call you back if I can find it. . . . Of course you can have it; what do the three of us want with a sewing machine?"

I hung up the phone and started making coffee. George came stumbling in; he had fallen asleep on the couch looking at pictures the night before and just stayed there.

"Who was that?"

"Martha Waylan."

"Ugh. What did *she* want?"

"Mamma's sewing machine."

"God."

George and I sat and listened to the coffee make.

"You okay, Susan?"

"Yeah, I thrive on death and family dysfunction. You?"

"I'm okay, I guess. I'm a little worried about you and Sam and, you know, old stuff. You sure you're okay?"

"Couldn't be better. Mamma's dead. It's August, not a squid in sight, and we're gonna find Martha Waylan a sewing machine for the church basement. Now, what would you like for breakfast? Bacon and eggs?"

"I sure would! Mornin', George!" Sam came in and flashed us both a grin. I fried six eggs, put them on the table with the bacon, and wished somebody's mamma would come back.

"Okay, Martha says we got to have this place cleared out by Saturday. Did you two finish everything in the garage? Martha wants Mamma's sewing machine. Did you see it, Sam?"

"I've seen enough of what I want out there. It's too damn hot for me. Ask George."

"I think it's pretty well finished, Suzie, but I didn't see a sewing machine."

"All right then, today we box up the house. Martha's sending somebody over with a truck on Friday. Sam, you go through the kitchen—save me Mamma's green mixing bowl. I'll go through the rest of Mamma's bedroom. You want anything, George?"

"Just the pictures."

■ ■ ■

I climbed the stairs again to Mamma's bedroom. It still smelled like her. I sat on the edge of the bed and fiddled with the bedspread Mamma had been so proud of. Sam came in. I knew he would. I sat still and waited. I watched him walk around the room, touching Mamma's things and saying nothing. I didn't think he'd been up there since he left Clydesdale.

Soon as Sam sat down on the bed, he began to shake. I knew the reliving that was coming and took his hand. His eyes got wide and his breath short. I reached out for him, and he stiffened. I stayed with him while he shook, and I waited for the old talk to start.

"No, Mamma. Please don't, Mamma. Mamma, I don't want to. I can't help it, Mamma. No, Mamma, no."

I held him tight until it stopped, and then I rocked him on the bed until his eyes softened, and he looked up at me. I wanted to kiss his lips and make it all better, just like we had done when we were kids. I wanted him to touch my breasts, because he wanted to, and because I *wasn't* Mamma. But instead we finally cried.

Twenty years of tears came tumbling out on Mamma's chenille pompoms.

■ ■ ■

Two days later the truck from the church came—and the men from the dump. We were finished with Mamma's house. George had mowed the lawn that morning, and Martha Waylan had been by to put up the For Sale sign.

Sam helped George get the lawnmower in his trunk, and I put the box of pictures up front with him.

"You take 'em, George. Make some sense out of it."

"Love you, Susan."

"Love you too, George."

"Love you, Sam."

"Yeah, me too."

George drove off, waving and hollering about calling us on weekends. Sam hauled the last box of stuff to my car and shoved it in while I went back to lock up. Then we stood on the gravel driveway and looked at Mamma's old house. It looked smaller somehow with Mamma gone. Everything did.

It Is Sunday

IT IS SUNDAY, AND, BEFORE I stir from the weightlessness of sleep, I know again with familiarity the ceremonies that will grace the morning hours. I can feel the early day upon my cheek and know, from the rising warmth, the colors that will be scattered by the window saints upon the dusty air of the cathedral.

The sisters, with whispered footfall, vigilant with their candles, will already be keeping watch over glistening rows of souls. Father John will light the incense, draping today's air with the ancient. Brother Thomas, in the loft, will be warming up the organ pipes—pumping feet and hands with equal vigor. The images of morning mass fill me with nearly a century of memories. Sleepily, I turn my whole face to greet the eastern light, bathing both cheeks in morning glory.

I finger through the closet in my mind, choosing carefully what to wear. Something special. I stroke the winter white linen suit and pass by the green tailored dress. I come upon the red satin almost hidden in the recesses of my faltering consciousness. . . . Yes, a perfect choice.

Organ music fills my ears. The beauty of it surprises even me, and I find my face damp with longing. The incense stings my nose with its pungent sweetness, and I raise my eyes to the dark wood of the kneeling rail. Oh, how I long to receive the Eucharist from the Father, to feel the red velvet crushed beneath my knees, to taste the dry wafer of promise.

I am so close . . . In a moment I will surely walk through the ornate doors and hear the echo of my feet upon the stone.

Slowly, I exhale and crack open my eyes. Cinderblock wall and aluminum bed-rail replace the cathedral of my sleep. Pictures from the great-grandchildren provide the stained glass within my institutional beige. The sharp odor of death that lingers with the aged awakens me fully, jolting me out of the Sunday morning I crave. Even my body conspires against me and resists my commands to rise. Soon, the nurse will arrive with my chair and wheel me off to tasteless eggs and black coffee. *Wheel of Fortune* reruns will be my morning mass.

Loving Joey

MADNESS HOVERED OVER US LIKE a hornet. Thunderstorms found the scared places on Daddy's face and just stayed there. He didn't say much those days, just kept working on that old truck. *That damn truck,* Mamma said. Sometimes I'd find her rocking and crying. Whimpering on that old green glider like a whippoorwill.

I kept me and Joey out of everybody's way. It seemed best.

We had lots of preserves that summer. Mamma canned peaches. Every single day. Said it calmed her nerves.

■ ■ ■

"Mamma! Joey fell in the road by Pa Gardner's place, and his lip's all swelled up."

"Good Lord, Joey! Let me see. Lida, get a cold cloth. I've got my hands in peaches, and the water's about to boil. Lord, child, but you do have a way."

"We were running away from the Wilson boys, Mamma, and Joey just tripped himself on one of them big old oak roots out front of Pa Gardner's place—"

"*Those* roots, Lida, not *them* roots."

"—and that's how he come to split his lip."

Joey sat still, like a good boy. I held the cold rag to his lip, and hummed so he wouldn't feel scared, and talked to Mamma for him.

Joey didn't talk. Nobody knew why, really. He said some words when he was little, but then one day last year he up and quit. Doctor said he thought it was the anxieties. Said some kids stutter when they're about Joey's age, and maybe Joey just didn't want to do that. Said we shouldn't worry.

Mamma had Joey's hearing checked by a specialist over in Clinton anyway. I could have told her what that fancy man did—Joey hears just fine.

"Joey's okay now, Mamma. Joey, you just go out on the porch and have a little swing on the glider. Mamma?"

"Make us some lemonade, Lida. It's awful hot."

"Sure, Mamma. Should I take some out to Daddy?"

"If you can make it look like a damn truck."

It was kind of funny, really. Or it would be if it wasn't your family. I had a Daddy who wouldn't stop fixing a damn truck, a Mamma who wouldn't stop canning peaches, and a little brother who wouldn't talk.

"Daddy?"

"Hmm?"

"I made you some lemonade, Daddy. Why don't you take a little rest? It's awful hot out here. Lemonade's cold. I put extra ice in it for you."

"Thanks, honey."

He drank it. Every last bit. Made me proud, too; I could see how he liked it. He even smiled at me. Smiled right at me and ruffled my hair a little. The scared places melted around his eyes, and I could feel how it used to be. For just a flutter—like the one breeze you'll have all day in the dead of August—the madness left. But then the glider squeaked, and Daddy looked up at Joey just swinging all quiet by hisself, and just as quick the hornets came back and shut out the sky.

They wasn't always so worried about Joey. Only just this summer it got bad. Nobody had any answers, and Joey just stayed quiet. It was like the goodness got all used up. Like all the bubbles disappeared with Joey's words.

Without the bubbles inside there aren't any more stories at supper. We don't run out the lane to catch Daddy coming home from the sawmill. Mamma doesn't sing. Daddy doesn't laugh.

I don't mind so much if Joey doesn't use words to say things. If you look at him, I mean really look, he gives you little telling things. Like the secrets you find in the colored pictures clumped together in the middle of the Sunday school Bible. I listened to Miss Delia talking Sunday-talk for years and didn't hear near as much about God as when I saw the picture of Jesus picking up that baby lamb.

Joey's eyebrows go up when he thinks something is funny, and, when he's scared, he licks his fingers. And there isn't anything as good in all the world as how he slips into your bed after a bad dream and slides his hand around your neck. So it isn't Joey's not talking that hurts. It's the other quiets. It's when the madness makes the air still, and you're afraid of the twister coming.

■ ■ ■

"Mamma?"

"What, Lida?"

"Can me and Joey go swimming?"

"Joey and *I,* Lida."

"Can Joey and I go swimming? I'll look after him real good, Mamma, and we'll come straight home if the Wilson boys are anywhere near. We won't be long, and I'll set the table as soon as we get back. That way you can finish your peaches without any bother."

"Okay, I guess. But wear your shoes, and keep to yourselves. I don't want to hear about any trouble from folks in town."

"Okay, Mamma. Thanks, Mamma. Get your shoes, Joey, we're going swimming!"

Joey and me smiled big bubbly smiles as we ran all the way down the lane. Swimming is the best thing God ever made, I think. When we got to the creek we stepped on the stones. It was already cooler under the trees. We didn't have to go too far before we came to The Spot. That's just what everybody called it. Everybody knew just what you were doing if you said you were going down to The Spot. The Spot was one of the prettiest places I'd ever been in all my life. The creek puffed out like a big belly and got deep enough to cover most all your body. The sides were slippery mud and perfect for sliding. There was this big oak tree with arms and legs that held you in. Its branches hung low enough to hang from, and one of the roots made a little ledge you could lay down across and dry off on.

We took off our shoes and all our clothes except our underwear. We laid them neat and flat on one of the scrubby bushes and splashed right in. I squealed, and Joey raised his eyebrows. We were the only ones there, which was good, 'cause everybody else in town was about as scared of Joey's not talking as Mamma and Daddy were. Joey and I took turns seeing who could hold their breath under water the longest.

We were in the middle of a spitting contest when I heard the Wilson boys come up behind us. I had been having so much fun I forgot to listen for anybody, and now it was too late. I had promised Mamma.

"Well, look here, Stan. Looks like we caught ourselves some critters down at The Spot."

"Sure did."

"Didn't you hear us over by Gardner's place, boy? We don't want no freaks around here."

"Sure don't."

"I don't know which one is freakier. The freak who won't talk or the freak who talks for him."

"Don't know."

"Either way, I bet we can make him talk and her shut up. What do you think, Stan?"

"Sure can. Can't nobody hear either."

"Let's see, which freak first? If we shut her up first, then he's bound to talk. On the other hand, if we make him talk, then she won't have to. What do you say, Stan?"

"The boy."

Joey was licking his fingers hard. Those Wilson boys started after him, and I heard myself scream. "Run, Joey! Run home, Joey! Now! Go! Get out of here!" Then I did the only thing I could think of—I jumped on Carl's back and started scratching out his eyes. I knew Stan wouldn't do anything without Carl, so I held on and dug in my fingers and kept screaming for Joey to run. But my voice got lost in creek water. I wanted to yell louder. I wanted to hurt those Wilson boys. I wanted my daddy to come and beat their heads in. I wanted them to die. But I was far beneath the water. Down where knees are supposed to be. The sounds were like under the covers in winter, and I couldn't see Joey.

I couldn't feel Carl, either, except for the big hand that was shoving my face farther and farther down. Then I heard Carl shouting something to Stan about Joey, and then everything went black.

Warm bubbles filled me up to the top like hot chocolate. The sky was blue, the air smelled like peach blossoms, and the grass was so green. So very green and soft to touch. I could hear Mamma and Daddy laughing on the glider. His arm was wrapped around her, and they were drinking lemonade. My lemonade. It was springtime, there weren't any peaches to can, and Daddy's truck lid was shut and sitting all alone in the garage. I couldn't see Joey, but I could hear him,

"Li-da."

"Joey? Where are you?"

"I don't know, Li-da, but it's beau-ti-ful."

"I can't feel you, Joey. I can't see you. Joey? Joey!"

"I love you, Li-da."

"Wait!"

■ ■ ■

I wore my best dress, Joey, the lavender one with the ruffles. Everybody else wore black. The Wilson boys got sent up to Clinton, Mamma quit canning peaches, and Daddy sold his truck. But I would give anything if you would have a bad dream and come back. Just slip into my room and slide your arm around my neck. You don't have to say anything, Joey.

In My Defense

WELL, I GUESS I JUST didn't like the way he smelled.

Sour, you know, like old citrus sitting on the ground too long. Foul. The kind of man that doesn't give a damn about anybody but himself. He had my kids, too. Snowed that goddamn judge into believing I was an unfit mother. Just 'cause he was a college graduate and had a job. Well, hell, who do you think got him through that? Me, that's who. But he got the kids, I got the trailer, and he moved into his mamma's house uptown by the River with both of my babies. Shit.

I can't say I didn't think about it plenty, but it's the God's honest truth I hadn't planned it out. He came over to tell me how he wasn't so sure he was going to bring me those children that weekend. He had them up at his mamma's and came out alone to the trailer park.

I had made a cake, special, for my youngest. It was her birthday. I remember it was pink with little flakes of coconut sprinkled on top. That Judy, she loves anything tropical. I made Henry a chocolate fudge one once. He said I was the best mamma ever. I had little cowboys on his; they were galloping on the icing like little John Waynes.

Well, that bastard just walked inside my house like it was still his own and sat down at the kitchen table. I knew what he wanted. He said, "I tell you what, baby, you give me a little cock suck, and I'll bring the kids over. "

I could smell his sour smell. It just hung around him, stinking up my kitchen. I guess that was when it come over me.

I smiled at him like old times and said, "Well, let me get on something pretty." I went into my bedroom and slid open the bedside drawer. Right there next to my Bible sat the gun he gave me for a wedding present. A gun for a wedding present. Should've known then.

I took my time. Put on a pretty Sunday dress, called for him to make himself comfortable, loaded the gun, suggested he get a cold Coca-Cola out of the icebox or something, and said I'd be right there.

I remember the way the sun was coming in the window. Slanted, like it does at the end of the day. It was butter yellow and summer slow in my bedroom that afternoon, and I could smell my own smell and not his. I slipped the gun in my dress pocket and stepped out into the hall. He was still sitting at the other end of the house. Sitting spread eagle at the kitchen Formica, grinning like a senator. I walked down the aisle of my trailer packing a piece in my best church dress.

I said, "Let me sit down for just a minute and look at what a big strong man you are before we start."

He curled his lip and said, "Take your time, baby."

He knew I hated him. He knew I'd do anything for my babies. He knew my weak spot was them children—only good things ever came out of that marriage.

So I sat down across from John Lee Curtis, put my hand in my pocket, and shot the man in the balls, right through my Sunday calico. His eyes got wide for a second, and the sound of gunshot filled my kitchen. He looked down at his manhood spilling onto the floor and passed out, slumped right onto my tabletop.

I watched him bleed to death while the shadows lengthened.

"Till death do us part, Johnny."

I dialed 911 and covered Judy's cake with Saran Wrap. Then I got out the Lysol and sprayed the air thick. I guess I just couldn't stand the smell of him.

In Glenville

I EAT ICE CREAM SANDWICHES when I feel all jammed up inside. I ate seven last night right after my brother phoned. I guess it's better than bourbon.

"Liz," he said, "you've got to make a visit home. Mamma's asking for you."

■ ■ ■

I love going to the health food store. There's this earthy cleanness that settles over me, and I just start believing I can be whole. That fresh smell alone can make me start up on all my positive thoughts. I head to the health food store about every six months or so, and then I have a good bulimic episode with my pantry. I toss out every evil box of sugared cereal and can of pesticide-ridden corn and fill it full of rice-flour waffle mix and organic canned tomatoes. It is a truly religious experience.

■ ■ ■

"Oh, Kid, is she bad?"

"Pretty bad, Liz. The doctor says she can't keep it up much longer—said to give you the word."

"I'll see about a flight. I should be able to leave by Wednesday."

■ ■ ■

When I was a kid, I loved August. August meant new school supplies. I just adored those white packets of paper all perfect inside their cellophane, the freshly sharpened pencils still warm and woody from the hand sharpener on the back porch, and the Crayolas. Oh, the Crayolas! Not one broken and all lined up in order like a regiment of hope. I would sit and touch their smooth skins and smell their waxy colors and arrange them just so in my pencil case.

■ ■ ■

"Damn it, Aunt Judy, I *am* trying to get there. This is the third time in as many months that everyone in Glenville is certain Mamma is going to pass on! That woman will outlive us all."

"Elizabeth Lucille Rainer, don't you talk to me that way. I used to change your diapers!"

■ ■ ■

I looked out of my apartment on Forty-fifth Street. All the noise and chaos that was so predictable comforted me. It never changed.

Every single day in New York City was gray. Every single day in New York City there would be too many people, too many cars and not enough taxis. There would never be a morning when I would look out my window and see a beautiful summer garden. There were no surprises to set my heart on here, and, if I wanted gardens, I got them myself. Jerry on the corner kept me supplied with fresh flowers, and Su-Ling had the best organic vegetables around.

I stood up, dressed, and made coffee. Then I called my agent.

"Hey, Rachel. Kid called again last night. Mamma's bad. Can you book me a flight?"

"Shit, Liz, you were just there. Can't those rednecks handle things for a bit?"

"Don't call my family rednecks, please. I will get the flight myself."

I hung up. Only *I* can call my family rednecks. I wasn't about to listen to some damn Yankee—who clearly didn't understand the gentility of southern family relations—insult my family. Even if it was Rachel. I grabbed the phone book and started crying. Why were there so damn many airlines, anyway? The phone rang. It was Rachel.

"Liz, don't hang up on me. I'm sorry. I'll have Cindi get you the flight. When do you need to leave?"

"By Wednesday. I'm not crazy, Rachel. She's my *mother*."

"Of course. I'm just worried about you. How long do you think you'll be gone?"

"Jesus, Rachel! I don't know—how long does it take to die? I swear, sometimes I think you have no heart."

"I just need to know for the flight information."

"Oh. Sorry. This whole thing has me crazier than a three-legged dog tryin' to chase his tail."

"What?"

"Never mind—something Mamma used to say."

■ ■ ■

I took my laptop even though I knew I would never be able to write while I was in the Carolinas. Still, I took it, I guess, because I could. I bought the newest, trashiest romance novel in the airport—I do not talk to strangers on airplanes. I rented a car in Columbia and drove down to Glenville and the land my family has lived on for generations. I rolled down the windows and inhaled. The humid earth spoke to my soul. I didn't know whether to laugh or throw up.

I met Kid at his house. There were dozens of children running around. Or so it seemed. Kid and Trula had four. They were beautiful, and it was summer.

"Aunt Lizzie's here! Aunt Lizzie's here!"

"Hey, sis, good to see you."

In Glenville you can go barefoot from May to October. No one in New York City goes barefoot. Except for the little black kids that play in the hydrants the firemen open up when the concrete begins to boil.

I watched Kid and Trula with their brood, and I wondered how they did it. How they lived each day without being terrified of those babies, of themselves.

"Oh, Liz," was all Trula said. She gathered me up in her arms and infused me with her warmth. "How are you?" And she really meant it. Up north they have this belief that no one really gives a damn when they ask you how you are. Not true in Glenville. Down here everybody knows your business. Asking how you are is their way of letting you know they've heard it all. It's comforting, in its twisted, incestuous sort of way. It's as southern as it gets, and, if you were born down here, you can never really get it out of your blood.

"Well, I don't know yet, Trula, and that's the God's honest truth. I either need a bourbon or a box of ice cream sandwiches."

Trula laughed and hollered, "Get Aunt Lizzy an ice cream sandwich, J. P.—Daddy put them in the back freezer."

"Can I have one, too?"

"And me?"

"Me too! I want one."

All four kids went running to the storeroom like otters chasing a red ball.

"Kid stocked you up with about half a dozen boxes, dear. 'No falling off the wagon here,' he said."

Kid smiled at me a little sheepishly.

"My baby brother is an angel, even if he isn't terribly subtle."

Trula laughed, and I hugged Kid a second time.

We sat out on the big front porch and ate an entire box of ice cream sandwiches, and I wanted to cry.

"Okay, Liz. Tomorrow we go see Mamma."

"Does she know I got in tonight? She won't let it go, Kid, if she knows I got in tonight and didn't come straight over."

"I won't rat on you, Liz. She's been really sad and quiet the last few weeks. I don't think she even has enough strength to bless you out."

"Oh, I wouldn't count on that."

Kid's youngest one left the sprinkler and came up onto the porch. She stood between me and Trula and put her soft little hand on my arm and smiled at me. She didn't say anything, just touched my arm and smiled. I was in love.

"Wanna share the glider, Abby?"

Abby nodded, slipped up next to me, and beamed with pride. She rubbed her cool cheek on my bare arm, and I thought, *If Rachel could only see me now.*

The sunset was beautiful. I sat on the glider with Abby, and drank sweet tea, and smelled the wet grass. Kid and Trula talked about summer vacation while the door slammed, and the kids squealed, and the sprinkler oscillated, and the neighbor's dog barked.

Finally it was dark, and Abby was asleep with her head in my lap. I carried her upstairs to her room, helped her into her nightgown, and tucked her into bed while Trula and Kid rounded up the others. I sat on the edge of the other bed with my suitcase and watched her sleep. I listened to the night sounds of crickets and children complaining about bedtime. I marveled at my brother and Trula—and at the loveliness of a home where children were put safely to bed.

The next morning there was strong coffee, fresh juice, a platter of eggs and biscuits, and enough sausage to harden a stout man's arteries. There were some things I still loved about the south.

After a noisy breakfast peppered with lots of questions and only a few arguments, Kid and I started out for Mamma's. Trula hugged us both and handed me a little plate of biscuits covered in Saran Wrap.

"For Mamma and Aunt Judy." She smiled.

"God, you are amazing, Trula. How did we ever manage without you?"

In Glenville, South Carolina, you always take a plate of food when you visit. In Glenville, South Carolina, you grow geraniums on your front porch. And in Glenville, South Carolina, you don't mention anything unpleasant.

Kid pulled up in front of Mamma's house. There were geraniums next to the door. Red ones in a large clay pot.

Aunt Judy answered the bell.

"Look who's here! My, my, it's our little writer," Aunt Judy announced. Then she whispered to me, "Oh, honey, I am so pleased.

You just can't imagine how I've had to handle her all alone. You don't know what it's been like."

I handed her the biscuits and kept my thoughts to myself. Kid squeezed my arm and grinned. He almost made me laugh.

Mamma was laid out in pink. Her eyes were closed, her nails were done, and her hair was up in a turban. She definitely looked like she was expecting me.

"Hi, Mamma. How are you feeling?"

Mamma opened her eyes and smiled. She patted the bed next to her, softly, and I sat down.

"I just want to hold your hand, baby. I just want to hold your hand." Mamma took my hand. Hers was soft and cool, and I wondered when it had gotten so thin.

"Bye, Liz," Kid whispered from the doorway. "I gotta go to work. Trula'll be by in a few hours to see if you need relief." Kid winked at me and left me with Mamma.

After a while, Aunt Judy stopped talking and went home. I let out the breath I had taken an hour before on the front porch and settled into the wicker rocker at the foot of Mamma's bed.

Mamma shifted in her sea of pink and opened her eyes. I went to her. There is a fierceness with which I love my mother. You can't spend years of therapy on someone you don't love. I wanted to crawl into bed with her and have her stroke my head like she did when I was a little thing and came into her room at night scared over some squirrel making a ruckus in the yard with the garbage can lid.

But Mamma closed her eyes again. It seemed too much work to keep them open. I studied her face and let things be.

Trula came by and fixed us BLTs on toast cut in triangles with Lay's potato chips and Coca-Cola in a bottle. We sat in front of Mamma's big console TV and watched *All My Children*. God, I love the south.

Mamma died during *As the World Turns* the next day, and everybody in town brought over a covered dish. I told Trula she ought to freeze some of them for later and was halfway through covering a plate of ham in cellophane before I started to cry. I just sort of crumpled onto the floor of Trula's kitchen with a plate of half-covered ham in my lap and let the sadness come. It came with laughter and with tears, and it surprised me. It came without the horror I had feared. It came quick and slow, and I knew that it would be over soon and last forever.

The Summer of My Tenth Birthday

IT WAS THE SUMMER OF my tenth birthday that I came to believe in God. It was also the summer that Sister Ignatius caught me pretending to have a twin. When she took me to Father Francis, she told him it was wrong for me to tell stories, but stories were the only thing I had. For my punishment, I was to copy letters out of the Twenty-third Psalm. Twenty-three times.

Sister Ignatius thought it was going to be a harsh punishment, but it turned out to be the most wonderful summer of my life. For two hours each day I copied beautiful words in the sweet-smelling room above the chapel. It was an oasis.

Afterwards I had to walk home, nearly wilting in the heat before I arrived at the little house I shared with my aunt on the edge of town. Aunt Tilley wasn't so bad; she had loved my mother—who was her younger sister—but hated my father for taking her away. My father was a writer and poor and bound for the big city.

Aunt Tilley took me in after Mother died. She never said what happened to Father. I don't remember either of them very well. Mostly, I recall Father reading us his stories. It was Aunt Tilley who insisted that I go to school with the sisters at St. Mary's in town. She thought it would cure me of my genetic tendency to exaggerate. She would have been mortified to know that it was on her account that I became a religious fanatic at the age of ten.

I loved the cool dampness of the cathedral. The winding stone stairs that took me to my room above the chapel were enchanted. I used to pretend that I was a princess from Italy or Paraguay and that, if anyone knew my true identity, they would mourn over not having given me more important rooms.

But truthfully, I loved Father Francis's reading room more than anyplace I had ever been in my whole life. The walls were lined with ancient books that had wooden bindings, gilded pages, and romantic titles like *The Love Poetry of Solomon* and *Laments from the Catacombs*. Of course, I had no idea what any of them were talking about, but I knew they were about things that could be felt and not always seen. I felt sure they were stories along the lines of those that sent me to my new paradise. Stories that somehow made sense of all the ugliness and pain I had already experienced in my short life.

I loved just being near all those beautiful holy words. I relished my new job of copying out the Twenty-third Psalm. I was careful to keep several copies done with a no. 2 pencil on school-gray paper for showing Sister Ignatius, but I spent most of my hours copying golden curlicues and elaborate script like the old books I had found. Somehow I knew instinctively that Sister Ignatius would not particularly approve of curlicues.

Father Francis turned out to be quite different. He surprised me one afternoon in July when I was so intent on my work that I didn't hear him come in. I was bent over a particularly difficult rendition of "Yea, though I walk through the valley of the shadow of death, Thou art with me," when he gently placed his hand on my shoulder. I nearly shrieked. Then I sat frozen in my chair, certain he was going to reprimand me for overindulgence. Instead, he smiled at me with a twinkle and nodded his approval.

After that, Father Francis and I were friends. By August he was reading me testament stories out of one of his golden holy books, and, before school began again, I had found my shepherd. I, a ten-year-old no one wanted, had found the Christ. By the time school started, I no longer needed to pretend I had a twin. I had Jesus and told everyone so. I heard that Sister Ignatius complained to Father Francis about my odd devotion to the Good Shepherd, but rumor had it that Father Francis told her to mind her own business and let me be.

The year Father Francis died, I was away at college studying to be a writer. I had nearly forgotten those early years in the cathedral tower and my burgeoning faith in God, when a package was delivered to my garage apartment. Inside, wrapped in a brown paper bag, was Father Francis's prayer book. A simple card read, "Father Francis wanted you to have this." I held the precious book to my face and smelled. The holy air of Father Francis's reading room still clung to the pages of his ancient book. I ran my fingers across the gold letters on the cover and looked inside. Several brittle pages full of childish curlicues slipped out onto my lap, and I began to weep as I read aloud the poetry of the Twenty-third Psalm written in my own ten-year-old hand.

She Had Prepared

IT WAS A DAY SHE had prepared for.

That morning she had packed their lunches. Last night's leftovers for Brian in a Tupperware, and the girls' school lunches in their pink and purple glittery boxes—the ones she bought them for no reason except that they were cute and she knew they would make the girls squeal.

Peanut butter and jelly. No crusts.

Grapes. Red ones.

Goldfish crackers. No preservatives.

Juice. 100%.

She hesitated a moment and put in a cookie. But only one each. It should be a healthy lunch today.

Once the girls left on their bikes for school, she tidied the living room and ran the dishwasher. The beds were made with fresh, clean linens, and a roast was put in the Crockpot—with baby carrots and onions for Brian.

"How come you're already making dinner?" Julia had asked when she saw her mother chopping onions during breakfast.

"Just want it to be ready for tonight, honey."

That seemed to satisfy Julia, and Marcy didn't seem to care; she was trying to wrestle the prize from the cereal box.

■ ■ ■

On the way into town she stopped and got the car washed. Brian would be pleased. He appreciated tidy things. Then she went to Luv Your Nails Salon.

"A pedicure and a manicure today, please."

"Pick your color," the Asian woman sang as she pointed to a wall of bright enamels.

She stood and thought how pretty the wall of color was. Tiny blots, fresh and new, ready to be used. She chose Melon. She liked the way its name sounded, and she thought it would complement her dress well. That was important.

The water was warm, and they rubbed her hands and feet and trimmed her calluses. She closed her eyes and felt pleased with her plan. They would be so proud of all the things she had thought of. All her care and concern would leave them in good shape. She imagined them happy without her sadness to pull them down. It made her almost glad. She rested her head back on the chair and listened to the music of the Asian women chattering to one another. In the background, Bette Midler sang, "You're the wind beneath my wings." Maybe she would finally be that for Brian and the girls. She had been unable to do so much. But this, this would help them all.

■ ■ ■

She swung by the cleaners and picked up her yellow dress. She felt a little sheepish; it was sort of fancy. She had bought it for one of Brian's office parties last spring. He had said she looked lovely. That's why she chose it; she wanted him to be proud of her.

The pharmacy was next door, and she picked up her anxiety medicine. Enough for the next three months.

At the bank, she took the money out of her secret savings account—the one she'd been slipping extra grocery money into for that cruise Brian was always talking about. She asked for a cashier's check and took it to Marshall's Funeral Home and made the last payment.

That was it.

■ ■ ■

She walked in the front door and hung her keys on the little kitty-cat holder the girls had made for her last Mother's Day. She called Brian and reminded him that he needed to be home early—before the girls got home—because she would be down at the Junior League helping out. It was the first Friday of the month.

He'd remembered.

She checked the meat in the Crockpot and lit a candle. Then she got a glass of water and her pills and went into the bedroom. It was a pretty bedroom: cherry canopy bed, blue floral coverlet. French Country, the woman at the department store had called it.

She opened the bag and the bottle and took out all the pills. She was glad they were small; there were so many. She swallowed them in fistfuls, and, when she was done, she stuck the bag under the bed. That wasn't so tidy, but she didn't know how much time she had. She slipped on her yellow dress, careful not to mar her Melon nails. She put on matching melon lipstick and folded her other clothes and put them back in the drawer. Then she lay down on the bed she shared with Brian and waited.

She had thought it would be peaceful. After all, it was anti-anxiety medicine. But she began to feel sick. She lay very still; she didn't want to vomit. She hated to vomit, and it wasn't in the plan. She checked the clock.

1:00.

Good. Brian and the girls wouldn't be home until 3:00.

Calm down, she ordered her stomach.

The sweats started, and she had to draw up her knees to keep from throwing up. She rocked that way, and prayed, and hummed, and tried to breathe like the yoga lady at the YMCA.

God, please help me to do this one thing right. Please, God, please.

She looked at the clock.

1:30.

Now she was shaking and sweating and sick, and suddenly she had to run to the bathroom.

Into the toilet went her hopes.

Dozens of little pills, almost perfectly formed, sank to the bottom of the bowl. She heaved and heaved until she thought she might actually die from the power of her own body. Against her will, it wanted to live.

She couldn't even die right.

She washed her face in shame and brushed her teeth. She took off her pretty dress and put the morning's clothes back on. She wadded up the frilly yellow casket costume and retrieved the pill bag from under the bed. She wrapped it all up four times in tall kitchen trash bags and put it in the bottom of the dumpster by the garage.

Then Adele Lee Walters, wife of Brian Walters, mother to Julia and Marcy, checked the pot roast, the time, and her face in the mirror, touched up her lipstick and blew out the candle. She got in her car and headed to the Junior League.

Eggs

THE BOX FAN PURRED IN the window like a giant cat. I kept my eyes closed and listened to Uncle Jim's mower chewing on Aunt Vi's grass. Everything around here belonged to Aunt Vi. Except me: I was only visiting.

Daddy left us, and Mamma went to a spa.

I pulled myself up out of the covers and put on my cutoffs. I was pretty sure Aunt Vi wouldn't approve. I smiled and left my bed unmade.

There was a note on the kitchen table. *Kitty, I have gone to the store. Uncle Jim is cutting the grass. Fix yourself some breakfast. I will be home soon. Aunt Vi.*

I drew out the old black skillet and lit the stove.

Uncle Jim kept on mowing.

I held three eggs in my hand. They might have been baby chicks. I thought about them all warm beneath their mother and waited for the cold skillet to heat up.

Uncle Jim kept on mowing.

The heat began to rise from the skillet, and the butter started to spit. I waited, wondering if Aunt Vi would get home from the market, if Mother was enjoying the spa, if Father was banging that blonde bitch.

Uncle Jim kept mowing.

Three babies. I held them in my hand all smooth and white. I cracked them one at a time and watched the skillet burn their skin and stood quiet while they fried to death.

The skillet started smoking, and the yolks got hard. I turned around, walked out onto the porch, and left them all.

The last thing I heard as I rounded the corner to State Road 489 was Uncle Jim's mower. From a distance, it sounded like a box fan. I kept my eyes open, swung my hips, and felt the fringe on my cutoffs tickle my thighs.

Mamma's Baby

MAMMA'S BABY LEFT HER TUMMY and went to be an angel before last Wednesday's potluck. It's making me have strange dreams. I keep seeing him, all pink and wrinkled, like Mrs. Tribbet's twins when they got home from the hospital. Except he is hovering around me on dragonfly wings, and I'm a frog.

Aunt Opal said Mamma went to stay at the state hospital over in Milledgeville. Aunt Opal said Mamma needed us to be brave. Aunt Opal said a lot of things except the one I wanted to hear.

"How long will Mamma be gone?"

"Oh, just for a spell, I reckon. Don't worry yourself, Myra. Your eyes get too big."

Aunt Opal doesn't have kids. She and Uncle Harry live over on Robert E. Lee Boulevard in one of the big houses. They have a garage, but Aunt Opal won't drive. Says she's too old to learn now, so she takes the bus to our house while Mamma is gone.

"Daddy, how come Aunt Opal has to come?"

"We need her help right now, Pumpkin. It'll be okay. Think we should surprise Mamma with a puppy when we go see her on Sunday?"

He tried to twinkle his eyes, but they made tears instead. We both knew Mamma didn't want a puppy; she wanted that little pink dragonfly baby that was never coming back. I hugged Daddy and said I thought a puppy would be lovely.

■ ■ ■

"George Robert Carlson, what in heaven's name were you thinking? A puppy!"

Aunt Opal stood in the kitchen with dishwater spilling off her hands onto the linoleum. Our new puppy was wiggling all around inside Daddy's arms, and both of us were smiling for the first time in days. Aunt Opal looked from Daddy's face to mine and then shook her dishy finger at Daddy.

"I do believe you got a piece of the devilment in you. Here I am, day after day, to keep this house running while my sweet sister is lying in the hospital, and you two come sliding in with a smelly old dog!"

Aunt Opal was shaking the dishwater all around by now, so she turned back to the dishes and steadied herself on the sink. Her words pinned Daddy to the wall, and he slid to the floor next to the puppy. Nobody was looking at me, so I picked up the puppy and went out onto the porch. There were no words in the house, and pretty soon Aunt Opal came out in her gloves and hat and walked down the street to catch the bus. From the back she looked like a chicken, her feathered hat bobbing up and down all the way to the corner at Jackson Avenue. She sat with a piano back on the edge of the bench, even though the bus wouldn't be by till seven.

I went inside and let the puppy lick away Daddy's tears, and then I made us ice cream with strawberries, and we sat outside for the whole sunset. The puppy fell asleep between us on the porch swing, and it was the best night since Mamma's baby left her.

■ ■ ■

Aunt Opal didn't come the next day, because it was Saturday, and Daddy didn't have to go to school. Daddy is the tenth-grade teacher at Milton High.

We slept in so late the puppy peed in the cardboard box. We washed the puppy in the yard with the hose and laughed and threw away the box. Daddy got a rope, and we tied the puppy to the porch and ate breakfast. Daddy fried eggs.

"Listen, Pumpkin, maybe your Aunt Opal is right. Maybe we shouldn't keep the puppy."

Daddy put the eggs on the table, sat down, and held his head. He seemed so small. Smaller even than the puppy. I didn't know what to say.

We kept the puppy on the porch most of the day, and, right before dark, Daddy took the puppy in the truck, and, when he came back, the puppy wasn't with him.

I dreamed all night about Mamma's pink baby and the puppy, both flying all around us on dragonfly wings. I sat on a lily pad and watched them up in the blue sky. The sun was shining, but the water around me was black, and I didn't know how to fly.

■ ■ ■

"Daddy, can I still come see Mamma today?"

"You bet, Pumpkin. It'll do her heart good to see her little girl."

I wasn't so sure. But I was afraid if my mamma stayed away much longer I would forget what she smelled like. I kept one of her nightgowns hidden in my pillowcase so I could be with her when I needed to at night.

Daddy pulled up the long drive that curved in front of the hospital. It looked like a big brick house—only bigger. I pinched the underside of my arm, sat up straight in my seat, and tried to remember all the things Aunt Opal had said that morning on the phone. I was so afraid I would croak out wrong words that I decided I would just hug Mamma and smell her real good instead. Daddy opened the door, and I slid out of the truck. The air was hot, and nothing moved.

"Judy Carlson?"

"Yes, Mr. Carlson, Judy is out on the terrace."

"How does she look today, ma'am?"

"Well, she ate some breakfast, Mr. Carlson, and let us wash her hair. She looks real nice. I think maybe things are looking up."

"Thank you, ma'am. I brought our little Myra along today."

"Good. Good! That'll be real nice."

She smiled at me, and her white hat nodded. Daddy took my hand, and it was cold and sticky like mine. We walked together to the terrace and Mamma.

I saw Mamma before she saw us. I saw the bandages on her wrists and remembered how awful red they dripped that day in the bathroom when she tried to leave after her baby. They dripped all over the bathroom floor faster and darker than Aunt Opal's dishwater could run off her hands in a fit. I remembered the sirens, and the flashing lights, and Daddy holding wet towels against Mamma's spilling arms and looking at me. His eyes were like the dark water of my dreams.

We got to Mamma on the terrace, and Daddy kissed her hand below the bandage. She smiled small and looked away. Daddy looked over at me, so I touched my mamma on the arm, soft, and she got tears in her eyes. Daddy knelt down beside her and held her cheek. Mamma looked at him, and I watched them find each other in little pieces and waited.

Finally, Mamma whispered my name, and I sat down beside her on the concrete bench and buried my face in her dress. She smelled mostly like medicine and strong soap, but, somewhere in there, she still smelled like my mamma.

She smoothed my hair, and stroked my cheek, and let go of her tears. Suddenly, we were all wet and tangled, and Mamma kept touching my face and saying my name, "Myra, Myra, Myra." Daddy folded me and Mamma into his arms, and we rocked in one great rhythm for a long time.

Later, on the way home in the truck, I reached out and touched the back of Daddy's hand. It was smooth and clean and strong. He looked at me, surprised—like he had forgotten I was there. Then he took a big breath and pulled me up on his lap.

"Wanna drive the truck, Pumpkin?"

I nodded.

There wasn't anybody for miles around, so we drove on the double yellow lines of County Road 24 all the way home.

Surviving Nashville

LAST NIGHT I SAT ON the living-room rug and cried. It was my thirty-fifth birthday, and all I could think was *My God, I can't do this for fifty more years*. I walked back through the sleeping house and stood beside each little bed. Lydia suddenly looked long to me, the bones in her face just beginning to widen into girlhood. Across the room, Mary slept with one hand curled beneath her cheek. In the next room, Drew lay in his loft—a chubby little boy with the mind of an ancient cleric, full of words too big for his tiny mouth to say. The baby was asleep next to Jack in our bed, and I stood motionless watching them both breathe gently—in and out, in and out. I counted seventeen breaths, went back into the living room, and let the stillness fill my ears like the rush of an ocean tide.

■ ■ ■

"Push, Meg, push!" I grabbed my knees and leaned into the

pain. I could feel the baby's head heavy and near. The sounds ran together, and the room blurred into a sunset. Eyes were on me; I kept pushing.

"Wait for the pain; don't push until you feel the contraction!" someone shouted. I think it was the midwife.

Jack was near, stroking my forehead, telling me the baby was coming. I threw up in a bedpan, and took a breath, and pushed as hard as I could. Suddenly she was there, all warm and wet and wriggly. I heard someone crying and singing at the same time. It was me. Jack cried, too. We wept as we touched her little wrinkled body. She smelled like new earth and felt like second skin, stretched lengthwise between my breasts.

■ ■ ■

Today I locked myself in the closet; I was scared of my own existence and the dark thoughts that pressed against the inside of my eyelids. I waited until the darkness of the closet quieted my mind, and then I came out and made cookies with the children. We walked to the park, and I laughed. Life is good. I can smell the sun.

Yesterday Jack and I went to the Outback Steakhouse. I love their caesar salad. I told him between the garlic croutons and the New York strip that I thought I might be going crazy. Then I laughed, like it was nothing.

The next day was Palm Sunday, and the children and I made flags of ribbon and sticks from the yard. We were going to have a parade for Jesus. I read them the Bible story from the book my father read to me. I loved my babies so much; it was only sometimes that I screamed at them. I didn't mean to. Lydia shouted at me that I looked like Ursula, the witch in *The Little Mermaid*, and I shouted back that I felt like Ursula! I stood in the bathroom for a while and ran water in the sink. I came out and asked them to forgive me. Then we ate grilled cheese. We left the ribbon and sticks and glue and scissors all over the floor, and we laid out a blanket, turned off the lights, and watched old movies from when Lydia and Mary were small.

■ ■ ■

I sat in the parking lot and breathed into a paper sack before I could get up the courage to go into the therapist's office. It was very proper and tidy, like any doctor's office. I filled out the paperwork like I was told. One of the questions puzzled me. It asked, "Why are you here?" I thought it was a funny question. It seemed to me that if I knew why I was there, I wouldn't have come. The therapist came to the waiting room to get me himself. I knew him from church. He smiled at me and ushered me down the hallway of bad paneling. It's funny what you remember.

He wrote lots of things down on a yellow legal pad, and I heard myself saying things I didn't know I had ever thought. I just decided to answer with the first thing that came into my mind. He asked me if I felt the sadness of my life, and I looked at him. No one had ever thought my life was sad. "No," I said. "I guess not."

■ ■ ■

I have been given an assignment. I am to imagine that the little girl I used to be is sitting in a chair beside me. Then I am to try to feel sad for her. This all came about because I told the doctor that I cried every time I went to the school to pick up the children. I cried at every school program and PTA meeting—just the smell of metal school desks and the sight of small children lined up together could bring tears to my eyes. I cried over my own babies—how

I was certainly ruining their lives with my inadequacies. But the doctor said I never cried for myself. He said that wasn't good. He said I needed to feel for the little girl I used to be.

What he didn't tell me was that the little girl I used to be might show up beside me in the Wal-Mart checkout line. He didn't tell me that she might suddenly burst into tears at the sight of a refrigerator magnet. Or that she would start telling my stories.

■ ■ ■

"Class, this is Margaret O'Sullivan."

I stood in the doorway and held up my chin. I looked at them all at once. They looked like a forest, and I felt like a very small squirrel.

A pretty girl with long, straight brown hair smiled at the teacher and raised her hand.

"How are we going to tell us apart?"

Everyone laughed.

"Yes, Margaret, I've already thought about that." The teacher turned to me, "You see, we already have a Margaret in the third grade, and you even have the same last initial. Her last name is O'Brien. Perhaps we can tell you apart by your middle name?"

I didn't say a word. The trees turned into grasshoppers, and a million eyes stared at me without blinking, like I was just a piece of grass.

"What's your middle name?"

"Anne," I whispered. I didn't want to be called by two names.

The girl with the long brown hair raised her hand again.

"That's my middle name, too."

The class laughed even more. My face got hot.

"My goodness, isn't that funny?" The teacher laughed. "Well, we can call one of you Margaret and the other one Margaret Anne."

The girl with the long brown hair didn't even raise her hand. "I don't want to be called Margaret Anne; I want to be Margaret, like always," she blurted out, glaring at me.

"Well," the teacher started, and, when she looked at me, I knew I had lost. "Since you are new here, why don't we call you Margaret Anne, and we'll just keep calling Margaret O'Brien Margaret. Now, everyone take out your penmanship books and turn to page thirty-nine. Copy these sentences in your best cursive."

I sat in the chair she pointed to and made my face plain. The girl beside me was the one with the long brown hair. I made a little smile at her, but she stuck out her tongue when the teacher wasn't looking.

The teacher handed me a book, and I turned to page thirty-nine. I stared at the long words with their loops and curls and couldn't breathe. I only knew *Ls*. In Tennessee, we had only just started drawing *Ls*. In Tennessee, my teacher read us stories while we lay on shag rugs. In Tennessee, I was the only Margaret, and my best friend had red hair. Short. Curly. Red hair.

■ ■ ■

I saw the doctor again today. We talked about third grade. He said most eight-year-olds don't contemplate suicide, but I remember standing at the top of the school stairs and imagining how I would look crumpled in a heap at the bottom—motionless, legs and arms bent at awkward angles, a small trickle of blood sneaking from the corner of my mouth.

■ ■ ■

The baby was absolutely precious. Creamy and sweet. The other three were playing under the table. They were Michelangelo. I had taped butcher paper to the underside, and they were painting the ceiling of the Sistine Chapel. I heard one of them squeal every time the paint hit them in the face. I only got angry a little, because I knew the paint would clean up, and it was keeping them busy. I put on some harpsichord music and nursed Zoë in the other room.

Peace only lasted a little while before Lydia came in shouting with seven-year-old indignation about how Drew had ruined the entire chapel because he didn't know anything about painting because he was only two! And certainly the great masters didn't have to be bothered with their baby brothers when they were on important jobs like ceilings and things!

Then Mary and Drew trailed in after Lydia, Zoë popped up from my breast looking deliriously drunk with mamma's milk, and the morning was over.

There they were—all four of them perched on my bed. It was only 10:30, and there would be no Jack until seven.

"Let's go to the park!" I said.

They squealed with delight, and I was only too happy to leave behind the mountains of dirty dishes and laundry. I grabbed some apple juice and a couple of diapers for Zoë, and off we went.

I watched them climb unfettered at the park and wrote poetry on a paper napkin that no one would ever see.

■ ■ ■

The late summer evening reminded me of lightning bugs and Tennessee breezes. I put on the Indigo Girls, and the children and I danced for Jack. We jumped and twirled in the evening light, and I put my arms over my head and spun my hips. I grinned sideways at Jack; he loved it. I felt the beer smooth me and giggled. The children enjoyed my play, and so we danced. Bare feet across the cool earth, arms and hair flying.

■ ■ ■

"What else happened in Tennessee?" the therapist asked.

"The summer between my second- and third-grade years, the locusts came. Did you know they come every thirteen years?"

He shook his head no and wrote something on his pad.

"They're born underground, but, when they finally come out, they die after a few weeks."

"I think I've heard of that."

"Every bush and shrub and tree in Nashville was full of them. In the mornings after breakfast, the women would come out on the front porch and sweep the dead bodies into the yards."

He waited for me to continue.

"I heard them singing the night my sister was born. Grandma Jean and I decided they had come to sing for her."

He studied me.

"I only held her once. She died before the locusts quit singing."

"That must have been hard."

"After she died, Mamma wouldn't go back into the house. We just left. Grandma Jean took me back to pack a suitcase. Daddy said I could only fill one because the movers would come later. Grandma Jean packed Mamma's. I made sure to get my Holly Hobby picture album and my white sundress. It had these tiny raised blue polka dots that you could feel even with your eyes closed—and a silky blue ribbon for a sash."

I left his office, got in the car, and drove hard. I got on the highway and drove harder. I watched every truck as it passed on the other side. One slip of the wheel, one tiny jerk. . . .

■ ■ ■

"Go straight to the hospital," my boyfriend practically shouted into the telephone. I sat on the other end and refused.

"I already threw up! I'm not going to the emergency room; they'll just laugh at me."

"You took three bottles of pills. Go to the hospital!"

"No!"

I hung up on him and sat on the hallway floor of the dorm, traced the carpet design with my fingers, and felt my breath in my mouth. It was still there. I was still there.

It felt like my head wasn't exactly attached to my body, and, if I tilted my head to the side, my eyes didn't follow. The clock on the wall said 2:12, and the hall was quiet with sleep. I decided to skip my early morning class, and put my head on the carpet, and closed my eyes.

When I opened them again, there were men in orange suspenders poking at me.

"Get off me! Stop touching me! Leave me alone!"

I screamed and screamed, but they held me down.

"You don't understand! I can't breathe. Stop touching me!"

Everyone on my dorm floor was standing in their doorways. They were all looking at me—huge locusts with bulging eyes. Their sticky feet burned my skin. I started clawing at my arms; the locusts were itching me. I heard a growl and tasted blood in my mouth. And everything went black.

■ ■ ■

I didn't have any of my children in hospitals. I hate hospitals. Hospitals are for sick people, and childbirth is a healthy, holy thing. I had my babies at home. All four of them. Little Zoë was a water baby.

■ ■ ■

I was curled up inside Jack's love. My head pillowed on his shoulder. We breathed in tandem. Mamma and Daddy were here this week. When they left, I cried all the way home from the airport. Later Jack and I made love, and as I came, I cried. I couldn't stop. Jack held me fast and took it all. He was amazing. I think maybe he is not from the same planet as I.

"Jack, am I crazy?"

"No, honey."

"But how can you be sure?"

"Because I've watched you with the children . . . the way you talk to them, the way you look when Zoë's nursing, the way you make their peanut butter and jelly. You're not crazy."

■ ■ ■

I sat in his brown office. I had to pay someone to talk to me.

I breathed slowly, but I was certain I sounded like the giant fan at the train station—the one that whirs and sticks and whirs and sticks—up in the corner where the wall meets the ceiling.

"Do you think I need to be here?"

I looked at him, and he realized I was serious.

"Yes, I think if you could have worked through this any other way you would have."

"So, I'm not just being dramatic?"

"No, Meg, you're not just being dramatic."

■ ■ ■

I was so excited, I didn't even care that I was Margaret Anne. My best friend Becky was coming to Virginia to visit me. I hadn't seen her in a whole entire year! Her mamma and daddy were bringing her to Williamsburg for summer vacation on account of its having historical significance. Daddy said we could drive all the way in to meet them and see the blacksmith and the tailor. And we each would get to make our own mob cap, Mamma said.

I was imagining what Becky looked like. She said she still had her hair cut in a pixie. I had a pixie, too, but I didn't like mine. Becky was cute with hers because she had curly red hair, but I hated mine because Mamma made me get it cut with my cousin last year. And I don't even like pixies. When my long hair was gone, Clay, the boy I liked, stopped chasing me on the playground and started chasing Cynthia because she still had long hair. Becky tried to comfort me; she said it made us more like sisters. I liked that.

■ ■ ■

The kids were looking at their baby pictures today. It was funny how they loved that. They would be happy for hours squealing over how cute they were "when we were little."

While the kids looked through their photo albums, I put the baby down for a morning nap and went to the china cabinet. On the bottom shelf, tucked behind my wedding bouquet and Grandma Jean's silver plate, was a small blue Holly Hobby photo album. Inside there were a few pictures of me from when I was little. I flipped through them until I came to a picture of me and Becky Goodwin standing in front of the fudge shop wearing our mob caps.

Lydia came over to show me a particularly funny picture of Drew covered in blue ink. While we laughed at him, looking like a blue hobo from trying to eat a stamp pad, Lydia asked me what I was looking at. Once they discovered I had pictures from when I was a kid, they all jockeyed for position to get a look at them.

"Who's that?" Lydia pointed to the picture of Becky and me in our homemade hats. Mary giggled with her thumb in her mouth, and Drew pulled the book over so he could see, too.

"That's a picture of me and my best friend, Becky."

"Cool!" Lydia said. "What grade were you in?"

"That picture was taken the summer before the fourth grade, but I only went to school with Becky for first and second grades."

"Why?" The kids looked at me, surprised. They didn't know.

"We moved from Tennessee, and I never saw Becky again—except for the time she came to visit me in Virginia. That's when this picture was taken."

They studied the picture. I looked at them all crowded together, intent on knowing the little girl I had been.

"Nana had a baby that died in Tennessee. A baby girl. She was born sick, and they couldn't make her better, and, when she died, we moved."

"That's awful!" Lydia looked at me in horror, and I felt my voice go a little shaky.

"Yeah, I guess it was."

Mary rubbed my cheek with her soft little hand, and Drew stopped pulling on the book for a moment. Lydia studied the picture again, gently. It was quiet, like the time we buried Mary's hamster.

■ ■ ■

All six of us were piled in the truck. Jack drove while I read *The Lion, the Witch, and the Wardrobe* out loud to the kids and passed out squirt cheese on crackers. We were on our way to Virginia to see my folks. The kids couldn't wait to see Nana and Pop-Pop. It was summer, and we were full of hope.

"Nana! Pop-Pop! We're here! We're here!"

The kids jumped out of the truck and ran up the hill to the porch. My folks met them in the yard; they had seen us pull up the long drive. There was a tangle of arms and legs as I watched my children wash my parents in love.

The kids ran in the yard, and Pop-Pop chased them. In between their squeals, he stopped and grinned at me from behind the peonies. Mamma hugged me, twice, and patted my arm. I breathed in the sugar maple and remembered my first poem.

Later that night, as I lay in my old rose bedroom, the familiar sound of the attic fan mingled with the crickets in the trees below. I watched the children asleep on their pallet; they were so beautiful together, like a song. I waited a moment to breathe, so I wouldn't miss it. Zoë stirred, and Lydia put her arm out. The smell of summer grass wafted across the bed, and I was every age I had ever been.

■ ■ ■

I sat in his office for the last time. I'm not sure how I knew. I just knew I would not be back.

I closed my eyes and thought about Zoë's sweet, sweaty smell, her tiny curls, moist with summer, clinging to the nape of her neck. I thought about Lydia, wise and strong and full of knowing. Of Mary, funny and bright with thumb-sucked hands. Of Drew, sturdy and certain and all boy.

"Sometimes," I told him, "I think I've found her."

He looked up from his yellow pad. He had always been kind and interested.

"She's the only one that shares my skin." I rubbed the back of my hand and found that I was far away. "The little girl I used to be is right here."

I showed him.

He nodded.

I stared at the floor and noticed how brown the carpet was. I felt my hand again, softly, and tasted the salt of my own tears.

Acknowledgments

THANK YOU TO my Mom and Dad for living with me so fully, and to Yvonne and Bev for gathering me in; to Todd, Brad and Jason for your stories; to Tawna and Carrie for your listening; and to Whitney, Meredith, Taylor and Olivia for putting up with the back of my head while my nose was in the computer.

Thank you to my dear Janos for being the midwife of these stories, and to Clare for your grace on so many evenings at Sol Terra; to Lorraine for your gentle guidance and encouragement; to Alice, Morgan, Clare, Peggy, Rhonda, Diana, Lisa and Phran for your deep faith, tender tears and delightful belly laughs; and to Mark Eddy and WordFarm for sacrificing time on your own art to produce mine.

About the Author

MAYBE IT WAS THE CONSTRUCTION paper or the modeling clay. Maybe it was the picture books her mother read to her as a toddler, or the A. A. Milne books her father read aloud once she started school. Maybe it was the dance classes or the macramé or the health food. Of course, it could have been that her grandmother was a painter, her great-uncle a Juilliard pianist, her mother a dancer and her father an unconventional minister. It could have been her brothers' antics over kick-the-can, or their Hobbit drawings or guitar songs, or the dozen or so dogs they had, or the absurd number of places she lived growing up. Maybe it was the ADD that they didn't have a name for in those days, or the depression that followed, or the struggle to find her own spirituality.

Whatever it was, Stacy was bound to end up as some kind of artist. She was performing professionally by the time she was nineteen, and she was directing, writing and creating interactive theater by twenty-four. Her first published words appeared when she was twenty-five, but it wasn't until she was in her thirties that she took writing seriously. After four kids, the theater turned out to be rough on family life, and so she began to keep the poems she scratched on the envelope backs that floated around on the floor of her minivan. She was thirty-five when a Mack truck totaled her Caravan, forcing her to give up theater and dance because of migraines and herniated discs. She turned to writing, promptly won a small pack of awards for her poetry and scripts, and, within a few years, landed a freelance job writing shows for the Disney Company. Since then she has published three children's books, dozens of scripts and the collection of short stories you hold in your hand.

Stacy was born in 1964. Currently, she lives with her husband, Todd, and their four kids—Whitney, Meredith, Taylor, and Olivia—in Maitland, Florida, where they've made their home for twenty years. When the house is quiet, she writes for Disney, or works on her new novel, or plays with construction paper for old time's sake.